Chris Hunter spent 34 years in enforcement, the last 28 years of which were in covert enforcement as a surveillance operative, and also as a surveillance instructor delivering training at the highest level. Additionally, Chris worked with elements of the security services and special forces in a training role.

Chris Hunter

SIERRA 22

Austin Macauley Publishers
LONDON · CAMBRIDGE · NEW YORK · SHARJAH

Copyright © Chris Hunter 2025

The right of Chris Hunter to be identified as the author of this work has been asserted by the author in accordance with sections 77 and 78 of the Copyright, Designs and Patents Act 1988.

All rights reserved. No part of this publication may be reproduced, stored in a retrieval system, or transmitted in any form or by any means, electronic, mechanical, photocopying, recording, or otherwise, without the prior permission of the publishers.

Any person who commits any unauthorised act in relation to this publication may be liable to criminal prosecution and civil claims for damages.

This is a work of fiction. Names, characters, businesses, places, events, locales and incidents are either the products of the author's imagination or used in a fictitious manner. Any resemblance to actual persons, living or dead, or actual events is purely coincidental.

A CIP catalogue record for this title is available from the British Library.

ISBN 9781035888979 (Paperback)
ISBN 9781035888986 (ePub e-book)

www.austinmacauley.com

First Published 2025
Austin Macauley Publishers Ltd®
1 Canada Square
Canary Wharf
London
E14 5AA

Table of Contents

Chapter 1: Berlin, British Sector September 1946	9
Chapter 2: The Ministry of Scientific Research, London September 1946	15
Chapter 3: Noirmont, Jersey, Channel Islands Present Day	24
Chapter 4: Jersey/London January	28
Chapter 5: Vandenberg Space Force Base, California	35
Chapter 6: The Custodian	38
Chapter 7: Corporate Trading International	44
Chapter 8: Downing Street	57
Chapter 9: Leaving Downing Street	63
Chapter 10: Scumbag Alley	69
Chapter 11: Vandenberg Space Force Base	86
Chapter 12: Highway 101	93
Chapter 13: The Karma Kickback	101
Chapter 14: Update	108

Chapter 15: Syria	112
Chapter 16: RAF Farnborough	116
Chapter 17: Briefing Austin	118
Chapter 18 Final Stages	120
Chapter 19: The Build-Up	123
Chapter 20: The Event	129
Chapter 21: Ho8	135
Chapter 22: Jayne Visits Ho8	140
Chapter 23: Ho8 Jersey, 1944	143
Chapter 24: Jersey Airport, 1944	147
Chapter 25: Arrival at Paris-Le Bourget Airfield, 1944	149
Chapter 26: Departure to Berlin	152
Chapter 27: Jersey War Tunnels Present Day	153
Chapter 28: RMPSIB Research	156
Chapter 29: Sierra 22 Depart Paris Le Bourget Airfield	161
Chapter 30: Tempelhof Airfield, 1944	165
Chapter 31: SS HQ Berlin, 1944	171
Chapter 32: The Basement Interrogation Level, SS HQ	174
Chapter 33: SS HQ Holding Cell	176
Chapter 34: Real-Time	180

Chapter 35: Berlin to Jersey	**183**
Chapter 36: London	**190**
Chapter 37: Burying Ghosts	**200**
Chapter 38: The Circle Is Complete	**205**

Chapter 1
Berlin, British Sector
September 1946

Pavel turned to Yvengy and smiled. They had just returned from some, well-deserved leave and had visited their wives for eight glorious days, during which Pavel had met his son for the first time. Several months before, he had discovered that his beautiful young wife was pregnant from their last few days of passion in December after Berlin had fallen in 45.

Yvengy had taken the piss out of him and counted on his fingers the months that had passed, joking that for the baby to be his, his wife either had the same gestation period as an elephant or she had been shagging behind his heroic back.

The smile he gave Yvengy was one of genuine friendship that had been forged during the hell of the last three years of the war. They had met during the defence of Leningrad, and suffered the torment of several of their mother country's winters as comrades at the sharp end.

The ability to make light of death and the loss of good, friends had saved their sanity, and now, here they were, agents of the communist state! He laughed to himself, agents of the

NKVD, the secret police, two hairy-arsed combat veterans not yet 25.

They had been selected for the NKVD in recognition of their distinguished combat records and their leadership skills as sergeants, leading troops in the field of honour. The mother country was good and generous and rewarded patriots, in this, they truly believed.

They were now on their first real covert mission in Berlin. It was just as dangerous as real combat since the city had been annexed into four sectors between the conquering allies: America, Great Britain, Russia and France. The political machinations taking place, now clearly identified their country's intention to have control over it all; despite the accord agreed to upon the defeat of the Nazis.

Both men had mixed feelings about what the motherland aspired to as they had fought with the allied comrades and had lost friends from their ranks.

Despite this, their allegiance would always be to Mother Russia and as such, they had prepared and planned this particular operation with care; more than once in the past forethought had saved their and others' lives.

What had it been that one of their British friends had said, "Time spent on reconnaissance is seldom wasted."

How true.

Pavel and Yvengy had been given the task of delivering highly sensitive material from a contact within the British-occupied sector of Berlin. The exact timing of the mission was theirs to decide but it had to be completed by the end of that week. They spent the first day, conducting a CTR (close target reconnaissance) of their planned route, both on foot and then, in a vehicle. They were familiar with the route and their contingency plans.

Having taken possession of the material that was contained in a robust fireproof strong box (similar to that of a tank commander), they drove along the first stage of their route. The cleared arterial road past the Brandenburg gate heading east towards Staatsoper. Both men were alert and checking for counter-surveillance.

Two miles into their planned circuit, the road ahead was blocked by a lorry which had struck a pedestrian who was now lying in an unnaturally contorted position in the centre lane. A small figure, covered completely by a hastily draped dark grey blanket that was absorbing the dark red liquid in which the body lay.

British troops were dealing with the traffic accident and tending to the driver of the lorry. He in an unsuccessful attempt to avoid the young lad who ran out before him, had braked too hard. Such that the vehicle steered away too violently and rolled the heavy old wagon and was now trapped within its crushed cab.

A younger boy (perhaps, the brother of the little shrouded figure, thought Pavel) was crying by the back of the upturned lorry. A British soldier crouched down beside him, his Lee Enfield 303 rifle at his side on the road as he held the little boy's sobbing and shuddering frame close to his, in a vain attempt to give comfort to the little soul.

In the background, the cries and screams of the driver could be heard as the first medics began to administer aid.

Pavel looked away thinking that the poor bastard of a driver would probably survive, condemned to spend the rest of his days as a legless cripple. The bitter experience of tending to injured comrades in battle had taught him that the quiet ones, unable to scream, needed help first, and an injured person who had enough time and energy to make themselves a pain in the backside by yelling, was well enough to wait their turn.

They both assessed that the accident was genuine and not a contrived threat to their mission. Pavel directed Yvengy to the left through a taped barrier across the entrance to the road and into a wide thoroughfare, which would serve as an alternative route into the more heavily bomb-damaged section of Berlin.

Pavel consulted his map and visually orientated himself to the coloured lines before him and considered their route deviation. The trade-off between risk and reward of taking this route was that it was, in fact, closer to the Russian sector and home and really, they had no choice.

As they turned into the wide rubble-strewn road, the wheels of the Volkswagen crunched on the debris. Pavel looked at the charred and derelict remains of Pankow, which must have once been a beautiful residential area.

Pavel was in fact, a deep-thinking, quiet-feeling man who marvelled in the wonder of life before the war. He had considered becoming an artist. He only came to recognise his own nature when he appreciated the beauty which grew from the horrors, he and Yvengy had witnessed as combat soldiers.

The gentle, graceful movement of the early morning mist which hid a milky sun full of promise for the coming day; the way the light would catch the dew hanging on a blade of grass as it moved in the slow morning breeze. He was just an ordinary man, who had been drawn from men who had families, hopes and dreams.

As the war progressed, he found that he was really not all that different from the Germans he fought against. Most were family men, enjoyed life and cried for their mothers in their final moments. He had seen so many of his comrades do the same.

In the end, he had ministered first aid to the Germans, the enemy, whereas before, like his fellow soldiers, he would have left them to die in agony—but really they were no different to himself or his friends.

They were all average family men, forced into this ludicrous nightmare borne from the sick mind of an evil man who managed to influence a generation, nearly to the brink of annihilation. How could one man's madness have caused so much ruin?

Yvengy cursed and Pavel smiled at his friend's impatience as the road narrowed due to craters on either side of the avenue. Yvengy slowly mounted a small mound of rubble, which was sprouting the first signs of grass and weed; the promise of life amongst all this death.

Simultaneously, the wheel compressed the rubble as it crested the mound and pushed down onto the trigger plate of an undiscovered German anti-tank mine. The detonator activated, and the front nearside wheel collapsed and accelerated into the interior of the vehicle; taking with it disintegrating vehicle parts travelling at several thousand feet per second.

The violence of the explosion ignited the ruptured fuel tank, and debris decapitated Yvengy as he drove. Pavel had only milliseconds to live, but time enough to experience the shock of his own death, before the pressure wave and heat from the blast vaporised his body together with that of his comrade.

Chapter 2
The Ministry of Scientific Research, London September 1946

He leant into his umbrella as the bitter wind drove a relentless rain onto every piece of exposed skin. His eyes watered as wind and rain conspired to blur his vision.

His raincoat bellowed as gust after gust threatened to rip the garment from his body and scatter the papers he held so preciously against him; protected only within the frail comfort of his briefcase, to the mercy of the elements.

Finally, battered by the gale, numbed by the cold, and breathless from the effort, he reached the door and sanctuary. The silence of normality that greeted him was deafening, and the warmth of the foyer made his chilled flesh burn. A gentle steam began to rise from his drenched mackintosh as he gently removed his sodden trilby.

"Good morning, Sir!" announced the man on the reception desk.

Cooper, a balding tubby man in his late 40s, was a bit of an in-house peculiarity in as much as he was a man, who despite the intellectual restraint that nature had placed upon him, was oblivious to this fact. He was more than willing to strike up a conversation with anyone that crossed his path. Unfortunately, the conversation usually recounted the same story or joke, a fact that people were generally too polite to tell him.

It was office lore that he could sense, anyone in the near vicinity of his desk and would intuitively home in, walking, as he did with a strange ramrod straight sideways waddle, not too dissimilar to a penguin, and engage the victim in conversation regardless of how rushed they were. A man of true rhino skin was Cooper.

To get away without offending Cooper was an art in itself. Most had indulged him, then as they became familiar with him, they feigned a hurried demeanour, and finally, as time passed, most took a circuitous route through the building to avoid reception.

A few brave souls even ignored Cooper, damning them for all eternity to his black book. Whichever road a person had chosen, the sad fact remained, that the only way into the building was past good old Cooper.

"And a good morning to you, Mr Cooper. You look and sound a damned sight better than I do!" replied Donaldson with affected bonhomie.

This banter had over the months led Cooper to regard Mr Donaldson as a genuine friend, albeit in reality, a remote and casual acquaintance, but a friend nonetheless, and someone, he wanted to give a good word to each day.

"Not to worry, Sir, you're in one of the only places in London left with decent heating. We'll soon have you dry, just in time enough to leave and get wet again!"

Donaldson suspected that nature had, in fact, replaced Cooper's intellect with that of an unconscious humourist. The trouble was that he was too often bloody right. The only thing dry at the moment was Cooper's humour!

Donaldson attempted to brush his wet hair into some semblance of normality, but instead, had to settle for a plastered lank mess, too drenched to do anything constructive with. Drops of moisture began to run along the lengths of his streaky matted hair and onto the shoulders of a very tired-looking tweed jacket.

"Oh, and by the way, Sir, there are two gentlemen from the Ministry of the Interior, awaiting your arrival. They are with Joan at the moment."

Joan was Donaldson's secretary. A fastidious lady, who enjoyed appearing older than her years; although by now with the passage of time, the reality was catching up with her pretence.

"Thank you, Cooper," was all that Donaldson could say. His heart was racing after the effort of his recent struggle with the elements as he tried to guess what lay ahead. "The Ministry?" he repeated to himself.

Life was so mundane now, since the end of the war, that this unexpected encounter with his old mob seemed quite interesting.

Donaldson passed through the outer office where Cooper had greeted him and into a long narrow corridor. His shoes squeaked as he made his way along the waxed linoleum towards the lift.

He realised, that he had been so preoccupied with his thoughts on the Ministry, that he had escaped the usual inane conversation with Cooper, that he had suffered for so long.

He filed the *Preoccupied Tactic* away as a countermeasure for future use against Cooper. He passed numerous doors on either side of the corridor, their panes of glass frosted, hiding whatever miracles His Majesty's government was working on.

His mind whirled in anticipation of the meeting he was shortly to have as he approached the lift. He drew back the heavily used and ancient Cowley concertina gate, and pulled open the wooden panelled door into the lift.

Donaldson often wondered if the engineer who designed this contraption had earlier in his career designed mousetraps. Because in God's name, how had the chap ever expected a person, such as himself, carrying his raincoat, hat and briefcase, to close the concertina gate before the wooden door closed on its spring-loaded hinge?

With adroit use of his left foot, enclosed in its church's handcrafted leather, he held the wooden door open as he locked and secured the gate. With no small relief, he withdrew his foot and allowed the spring to do the rest for him.

As the lift rose, he wondered what could be so important. It was barely 8 o'clock in the morning. He pondered whether it could be some of the German Intelligence documents that his friend Reynolds had been translating whilst they had served together at Bletchley Park, the secret crypto-attack facility; which had had such astounding success against the German Enigma encoding device during the war.

Donaldson was still proud of the achievements of Bletchley under the inspired leadership of brilliant mathematicians such as Turing. Donaldson was unaware of the revere, in which, he too was held by his colleagues for the contributions he had made to the decoding of Enigma, and being almost painfully modest by nature always sold himself short in his achievements.

However, this somehow added to the mystique that others wove around him and created an aura of confidence and professionalism that made others regard him as a natural leader.

The juddering of the lift shook Donaldson from his thoughts. He watched the darkness of the lift shaft pass into the light of a new floor before fading again like the dawn and sunset of a whole day in seconds. Finally, the lift slowed, and rose slowly above what he determined was the floor he wanted, before coming to rest gently and level with floor 10.

Donaldson, then in reverse, performed the same contorted ritual to escape the mousetrap. He vowed that he must use the stairs in future. There was talk that exercise as simple as walking upstairs promoted better health.

As the door to the lift closed, Donaldson was already heading along another linoleum-waxed floor to his office. As he approached the double doors into the outer section of his office, which Joan occupied, he spied through the frosted glass the seated figures of the two men waiting for him to arrive.

His curiosity increased, he opened the right-hand door and was greeted by a warm smile.

"Good morning, Mr Donaldson," said Joan. "Mr Cartwright and Mr Godfray have arrived to see you. I explained to them that you had meetings scheduled for this morning, and papers to read beforehand, however, they were most insistent." Joan turned her head towards the two men as she spoke, but only slightly enough to convey her disapproval of their intrusion into her organised and meticulous kingdom.

Mr Cartwright unwound himself from a low chair and stretched as he stood. He was a distinguished-looking man in his late 40s, but still athletic. His hair was cut short, in a military way, which showed sparkles of grey as his hair was caught by the stark light bulb overhead.

His face betrayed the look of someone who had served his country at the sharpest end. He was clearly relieved that he had an excuse to extricate himself from the confines of the so-called office comfy chair.

Donaldson watched Cartwright as he stood. During his time at the crypto-attack centre at Bletchley, he had himself been in the same crumpled state, where the task at hand had dictated just how dishevelled your appearance became.

Donaldson appraised the situation, a concentrated intent expression on his face. "Joan, please bring tea through into my office for Mr Cartwright, Mr Godfray and myself. And I would appreciate my diary being cleared, at least, for a couple of hours."

Donaldson turned to Cartwright and said, "I have the feeling that what we have to discuss is very important."

Cartwright pinched the bridge of his nose as if the act would keep him awake. "You could say that, Mr Donaldson."

Donaldson noted the guard's tie and the generic accent, which accompanied it.

An officer, he thought. *Two I bet, Godfray appears to be of the same mould.*

They entered Donaldson's office, Godfray following Cartwright. Cartwright sat as Godfray closed the door carefully and checked its security before taking a seat beside him. Both were travel-worn and tired.

"Gentlemen," Donaldson began. "I can read the signs, but I would appreciate some indication of your background and authority."

Cartwright smiled, thinking to himself that Donaldson was every inch the professional he had been briefed to expect. He handed over a letter of authority signed by the Prime Minister himself. Donaldson studied it. He placed the letter down carefully on the leather surface of his mahogany desk and turned to Cartwright.

"Colonel, I must say you and the Brigadier, are rather senior to be your run-of-the-mill messenger boys."

"If I may, Sir?" Godfray said to Cartwright.

The Colonel smiled and gave a weary nod as he waved his hand for Godfray to continue.

Godfray took a breath and paused as if preparing to deliver a speech, rehearsed but as yet unperformed. "We believe that we have uncovered some extraordinary material from archives seized from the Gestapo. The fact that we came into possession of this information is pure luck, as the car carrying the material was destroyed by an undetected mine in Berlin en route to a forward Russian checkpoint."

"The vehicle had been travelling from our sector. It turns out that the driver and passenger were Russian NKVD officers engaged in a clandestine operation. We would have remained blissfully unaware of the ruse, had they not met with such an untimely demise."

Cartwright grunted and said, "Bloody untimely for them, bloody lucky for us!"

"Absolutely, Sir," Godfray agreed. "Anyhow, the fact that they were removing material that had not been authorised under the agreed treaty of the occupying forces of Germany, specifically, from the British controlled sector, has caused much consternation, behind what Mr Churchill has quite rightly phrased the *Iron Curtain*."

"As I am sure you are aware, the Russians are playing a rather tasteless game at the moment, and have made clear their intention to annex Berlin."

Donaldson nodded as he thought back to the innocent days when he had worked alongside some of the finest mathematical minds in the Academia of Cambridge—Russians who were now considered potential enemies. He had truly liked the eastern Europeans he had met and counted some, like Symenov as a true friend.

They had so recently been our allies and had spilt their national blood together, ridding the world of unbelievable evil that had threatened the very humanity from which mankind had derived the adjective to describe themselves. What was happening to the world?

The world was evidently still in bedlam. Ultimately, he had to acknowledge that whilst the individuals he once deemed trustworthy had fallen short, he must now rely on the judgment of those who possessed all the facts. Unlike him, who saw the world through a limited lens, they could offer a clearer perspective on the truth.

Cartwright had been watching Donaldson as Godfray delivered the script. Part of his brief was to play the tired soldier, to allow Donaldson to relax and forget about him whilst focusing on his subordinate. For Cartwright, the tired part was not an act.

Cartwright had been chosen for this role because he was an honest man and a natural judge of character. He observed the maelstrom of emotions cross the face of Donaldson as

Godfray was delivering the tip of what was a very large iceberg.

He also clearly saw the simple patriotism that burnt through the fog of sentimentality, and noted with relief, that his briefing had been accurate. They could trust the man sitting before them. What remained now was, how the hell do you break something of this magnitude to someone?

Chapter 3
Noirmont, Jersey, Channel Islands Present Day

The little electric blow-heater whirred as it had done faithfully since 03:30 that morning, an unnecessary backup to an efficient central heating system in a well-insulated home; the result was stifling. The bedroom was overheated and was becoming hotter as the sun broke through the scuddish cloud, bathing the cottage in a milky light.

The cottage had stood on the site for over three hundred years; the mixture of deep blue granite, soft pink and subtle mellow brown hues of the stone created a splendid façade, held together with creamy lime pointing.

The beautiful rustic stonework now embraced the sturdy oak beams which ran across the ceilings, supporting the floors above, and other beams which ran around each door frame; lintels which now, through age, were as strong as iron.

The natural wood doors were the same ones the original builders had installed during the reign of Elizabeth I. Time and the settlement of the foundations had made the doors and their frames become out of square in a lopsided way that only added to the charm of the cottage.

Each door was itself set in what appeared to be a recess but was, in fact, a three-foot deep wall that separated each room. Building design back then worked on the theory that if it looks big and sturdy it won't fall down.

The fact that the cottage was still standing when others after it had been built, then lived in, then fallen into disrepair and then, finally demolished, bore testament to the logic of a bygone era.

In the lounge and master bedroom, the eye was drawn to huge ancient fireplaces that dominated the gable-end walls and formed the centrepiece of each room. These features alone made the cottage a much sought-after property and should have been a home anyone would have been desperate to enjoy. Alas, not anymore.

A gap in the curtains of the bedroom enabled the angle of the morning sun to create a direct path across the face of a sleeping but restless form. The body's chemical reaction to sunlight on the eyelids led to cortisol hormones responsible for the waking process being released into the body's system.

Slowly but surely consciousness rose through a muddled fog of alcohol and fatigue. Sleep was deserting a sinking ship, much in need of a safe haven.

The heat and dryness in his throat worsened the throb of a headache and the stifled breathing brought on by the heat-blocked nasal passages. Carter wanted to lay in a cool place, in the dark. His alimentary canal shook in a brief spasm as he remembered the neat whisky he had drunk; he prayed to be sick and to be left alone.

Finally, it could be put off no longer. He flung the duvet back, briefly enjoying the relative release of hot air and the comparative coolness that its removal brought.

He rolled to his left and placed his feet on the sumptuous green carpet, resting his head in his hands as if to prevent it from pitching and rolling, which he knew would only lead to a surge of pain as the throbbing increased.

Luck was not with him as the slight momentum of sitting up led to a blanket of intense agony descending over him. His parched vocal cords could only croak in protest. The surges of pain seemed to squeeze his head and wash over him in wave after wave of nausea; sluggishly sloshing through his body in rhythm with the soon-to-be-released vomit in his belly.

His salvation lay in the en-suite bathroom a short crawl away. On all fours, he lunged the final few feet to the toilet and puked down the bowl. The act of his belly wringing the foul liquid from his gut only caused another wave of pain.

This time, his throat had been moistened by the departure of his stomach contents, and he let out a long groan between the tears of agony through eyelids squeezed closed. The aftershock and shudders of the real and the phantom retching left him clammy and dazed.

Finally, like a baby deer trying to stand on ice, he managed to crouch over the sink, turn on the cold tap and feel the freezing water cascade over his head and neck.

"I may just live, and I swear, I'll never do this again," he promised to the plughole and promptly vomited into his newly found confessor.

This act left him weak at the knees and bereft of all strength, he collapsed onto the carpet and lay against the base of the toilet.

For a long time, his head rested against the cool ceramic below the water level of the toilet. A few minutes after flushing a toilet, full of sick on its journey to wherever the gurgle of the water refilling the flush subsided into a peaceful trickle and finally, into an absorbing silence within the total darkness of the toilet.

He shuddered as a spasm of memory flooded through his body, and then finally, a peace of sorts settled onto his prostrate form as he shivered; embracing the trunk of the chilled porcelain against his temple.

He pulled an oversized towel from the rail above him; warm, reassuring and cosy, then sleep descended, enveloping his form in a warm cradle and pain and nausea faded into the blackness of oblivion much prayed for.

Chapter 4
Jersey/London
January

The decision had been made. Based on shopping receipts and cashpoint withdrawal slips recovered by the Germans from Carter's personal possessions, it was clear that he had been captured just weeks in real time, synchronically before D-Day.

It was now more than ever necessary to explore any avenue to try to find a trigger for what lay ahead. And so, Carter's home address, his car, his mobile phone, landline and financial affairs were to be the subject of an intrusive operation.

Authority had been granted by both the Home Secretary in the United Kingdom and the Attorney General in Jersey, Sir Robert Le Maistre.

It was quickly established that Carter and his wife were going to London for a midweek break to catch a show and relax. This would be the opportunity for the government agencies to crack on.

Carter's house would be the subject of a CME (Covert Method of Entry). Whereby, with lawful authority, highly skilled operatives of His Majesty's government would break into the house, and place intrusive devices such as cameras and covert microphones for live monitoring by an intelligence team back at GCHQ.

Similarly, Carter's car would be rigged with a tracker, or a *lump* in the parlance of covert operations and hard-wired into the vehicle battery supply to save having to change the covert power system every few days; therefore, reducing the risk of a compromise, especially, considering Carter's background.

With the knowledge of the hotel booking at a very prestigious London hotel (that was very sympathetic and accommodating to the security services), Carter was allocated a suite which had been, upon notice, CME'd and was good to go; ready and prepared for the arrival of the Carters.

The logistics were enormous. Nothing could be left to chance or placed in jeopardy by corner cutting.

The responsibility for pulling all of this together was Mike Johnson, a super smart spook from MI5 who looked like a second row in rugby.

Mike took to the stage at the briefing area at the Joint Intelligence Agency Group at Chicksands precisely at 12:00 hours. At 14:00 hours, following questions, his work on stage was done.

In short, Carter would be followed from his home address to Jersey Airport. At the airport, two surveillance operatives from Jersey would also be passengers on his flight to ensure he arrived, as advertised. At London Gatwick, another would be flown ahead on the preceding Gatwick flight to identify Carter as a backstop, in case, he somehow, slipped the team on the aircraft once they had disembarked airside.

Jersey is a major international finance centre with genuine and impeccable regulatory controls but still struggles to shake off the *tax haven* status peddled by its competitors; that aside it meant that travel between Jersey and London was significant and provided numerous flights between both destinations on a daily basis.

This busy hub of global finance meant private jet clients and business travellers were annually in the tens of thousands enjoying the prosperous financial environment in this offshore paradise.

Once at Gatwick, Carter would be surveilled through from airside to landside, and once clear, the Jersey team would hand the live operation across to an awaiting United Kingdom surveillance team.

At that point, the operational order covered all reasonable movements the subjects might make as the surveillance team would not know how Carter would leave the airport. It would be either by car, taxi, bus, rail or the Gatwick Express.

Sounds easy on paper but a fucking nightmare if you are the ground commander in charge of the team with options requiring different tactical control measures depending on which means of transport was taken.

The surveillance team, therefore, deployed to meet and greet at passenger arrivals. Operatives were tasked to cover movement towards the Gatwick Express and trains. Others were to cover taxi and metalled road public transport movements (the latter being an encompassing term for roads made of concrete, bitumen or other man-made constructs; the term itself was derived from the Latin word Matallium—to mine or quarry as opposed to a farm track).

It is more of a military term which had crept across into covert enforcement.

As it turned out, the Carters walked past the HMRC Border Force Control and straight onto the Gatwick Express. The other operatives held their positions until the doors closed and the Express moved away.

Although, highly unlikely in this case, a subject using counter-surveillance methods would get on the Express and then disembark the train at the last second and strand any surveillance operatives on board. Hence, it is the reason the wider team never broke cover until the subject was confirmed on the train.

This counter-anti-surveillance tactic is applied to all forms of public transport the subject may use.

At that point, the subjects were confirmed on board the Gatwick Express, the remaining surveillance team who were not tasked with keeping the subjects under control were none too dissimilar to a swan; gentle and graceful above water but going like the clappers out of sight below. They needed to get to one of the team's vehicles or risk being left behind.

The surveillance officers quickly and covertly made their way to the nearest mobile unit (probably not the one they deployed from). With no small sense of relief at being collected, they then left at speed to London Victoria in support of the team that was ahead and waiting to take Carter (Subject 1) and Callie, Carter's wife (Subject 2) as they were now known to the team.

Mike Johnson preferred the old designation of *Target* as opposed to *Subject* as it carried more punch. The reason the terminology had changed was as bizarre as the circumstances surrounding the case, that was the catalyst for the change.

In short and many years ago, an armed Metropolitan Police surveillance team known as a MAST (Mobile Armed Surveillance Team) had been following a male armed robber who was referred to as the *Target*.

As bad luck would have it, the *Target* was shot a number of times by the surveillance team. Months later, in court, it was suggested that it was always the Met's intention to shoot the individual as they had called him a *Target* and surely, that's what you do to a target—shoot it!

Much flapping occurred within the politically correct police senior command circles and the operational reference name was changed from target to subject. A truly stupid knee-jerk reaction in an attempt to placate criticism and to be seen to be self-righteously critical. Virtue signalling at its finest.

Jamie since arriving at Gatwick had felt his antenna twitch. Nothing solid, just a sixth-sense thing which he acknowledged from his time in the field, but put to one side as he was on safe ground.

The half-hour ride into Victoria was relaxed and Jamie and Callie chatted and laughed, almost like teenagers in love, oblivious of the outer world around them.

As the Express entered Victoria Station, the operative on the train gave rapid clicks on their PTT or press-to-talk clicker. The PTT looked like a car fob, as it was intended to and was not physically linked to the operative's personal body set as they were in the old days when they would sometimes be hidden in some quite imaginative places.

The awaiting team was callsign Alpha. Upon hearing the rapid clicks, the Alpha unit who first heard the transmission would relay it from the sets in their cars.

"Alpha 4, to the team, rapid clicks. Stand by! Stand by! Stand by!"

"Alpha 3, foot (*foot* is a term used to differentiate an operative on foot from a vehicle) can confirm that the Express is about to halt at the station platform. The Express is slowing and has halted at its platform."

"Delta 1, foot (the operative on the Express who had given the rapid clicks) has the eyeball. The subjects are exiting the Express and are on foot towards the egress of the station."

"Alpha Commander, to the team. Stand by! Stand by! Stand by! All units acknowledge in sequence."

The Alpha units and foot operatives did so, some 20 operatives in total. Some were dressed as Big Issue sellers. A couple were driving taxis (perfect for picking up teammates), another was dressed as a vicar, and another a fake pregnant mum; all part of the bland demographic of the team.

The fat chubster in his hi-vis, chomping on a burger next to you was probably a highly trained operative; there were very few blue-eyed, statuesque surveillance officers out there. Too showy and memorable.

In surveillance, there were two points that boiled down the essence of what the craft of surveillance unequivocally demands. Could you be recognised, remembered or described? And ego aside, if the next move was to show out, pull out.

And so, the team were dressed to blend in and be bland. Frequent changes of foot personnel meant a surveillance officer would only once follow the Carters into any premises, café, bar etcetera before being rotated back to their vehicle. If, for some reason, they had to deploy on foot again, they would do so with a complete change of appearance.

You could not wear the same clothing twice. For this very reason, a fresh team would deploy each day, so as not to risk being recognised or remembered.

Sadly *jobs* had been compromised by the body language, movement or subconscious habits of a surveillance officer. Even watches and jewellery which are worn by second nature to the wearer had been pinged and caused the subject to abort their plans.

This is why, any operation costs huge sums of money and is not given the green light easily.

The Carters arrived at the hotel and checked in. Even in CME operations, private moments were recorded but respected and as such, were not reviewed or listened to in real time but could be, if necessary. So, that accounted for that first afternoon.

So, over the Carters' three-day visit, a new team was entrusted with the burden of the operation, so as not to potentially cause a compromise through sublime or overt recognition. A good call, all things considered when following someone like Jamie and his wife.

In general, the scumbags who end up in the spotlight of a surveillance team are most aware of three points. On their way to commit a crime, at the point they do, and then, when they leave. Even the most switched-on lacked the ability to be surveillance aware all day, each and every day; it would simply be too draining.

At some point, anyone would fail under that intense scrutiny and revert to their natural type and become compromised.

Chapter 5
Vandenberg Space Force Base, California

The United States Space Force was a newly created branch of the US armed forces, officially coming into existence as a military entity on 20 December 2019, and was organised under the Department of the Airforce in the same way the US Marine Corps comes under the Department of the Navy.

The Titan IV launch vehicle that sat on the launch pad was at the home of the 30th Space Wing.

A steady drizzle covered the sky for miles around and made the wet leviathan glisten with the menace of a waiting predator. The powerful three-stage rocket was capable of placing 47,800 pounds of hardware into a low-Earth orbit, or in this, case a KH-12 satellite with a total mass of 612,990 kgs.

The mission was unlike any that had been undertaken before. An elaborate cover story had been prepared in order to disguise its true purpose to the hundreds of personnel involved in the development, research and execution of the operation.

The USSF, in conjunction with NASA, was publicising the launch as a scientific deployment, which would primarily benefit the United States Geological Survey in studying the gradual shift of the European continental shelf and its effects on the sea's thermo-cline layers.

The payload purported to be on the Titan was one of a line of TIROS satellites used by the National Oceanic and Atmospheric Administration (NOAA).

The payload was, in fact, a modified KH-12 surveillance satellite carrying a huge amount of mission-specific hardware. A multi-billion-dollar payload primarily designated for a one-stop mission. This cutting-edge piece of technology was the jewel in the crown of surveillance satellites.

This was a very strange use of a KH-12 surveillance satellite and even more so, since it was going to be placed in a geostationary orbit in keeping with the operational cover story given out by the USSF and NASA.

Importantly, so as to maintain the credibility of the disinformation, the deployment had to provide the USGS and NOAA with the product they were expecting.

This led to the billion-dollar development of a hybrid satellite, which was in the main a KH-12. But just as importantly, it had the NOAA capability to provide an array of scientific data-gathering instruments. The number of these were not advertised for launch for several years.

But they were a combined NASA and Stanford University project specifically designed to examine advanced research into emerging theories in physics, derived from the now-venerable relativity theory. Also, were a part of the quest for the *Theory of Everything* (ToE) which was the scientific equivalent of the Vatican's search for the Holy Grail.

To the believers, it was out there somewhere, and in reality, the net was closing and what was more important was that a deadline was approaching. That, if not met, could have catastrophic consequences for mankind. Stanford was unaware, that NASA had developed the project to this extent. NASA wanted it to stay that way.

Chapter 6
The Custodian

The deployment of the hybrid KH-12 was the culmination of an intelligence operation, which had been initiated in 1946. It was one of the few black (ultra-top secret) operations that had not been compromised on either side of the Atlantic through subversive espionage, social engineering, greed or bragging.

This was not a result of particularly credible security, but brutal paranoia. In essence, if any individual holding a ministerial or presidential role, or any other government or civilian position, was entrusted with even a small portion of sensitive information and later deemed a security risk—whether directly or indirectly—they were eliminated.

The lonely and difficult task of sorting the wheat from the chaff, initially, rested with the custodian who held the responsibility of conducting the threat assessment, based on the intelligence material and collateral data.

The custodian held the necessary authority to action the required resolution once the degree of compromise had been assessed. But sometimes, the custodian was outvoted, and the cost was lives.

Only a small number of individuals had held this most onerous and challenging post since the end of the war. David

Mallory was the present incumbent and had carried out his duties for the past 15 years with the utmost integrity.

Intelligence generally requires no evidence and is assessed against other data held by a number of intelligence agencies, friendly or otherwise.

All intelligence is then graded against the 5x5x5 matrix based on three principals and their subjugated five sub-determinations; the headings being Source Evaluation, Intelligence Evaluation and Source Handling Code.

This cloudy soup of de-facto intelligence, the source credibility, the source history and the timing of the receipt of the intelligence is given to intelligence analysts. They are experienced field operatives and highly intelligent and savvy people.

They are expected to supply the intelligence community with watertight operational intelligence (quite often under pressure and the subject of judicial scrutiny months later) and rarely did they have on their side someone who could realistically manage the expectations of their military and/or intelligence *customers*.

Sometimes, *corrupted data* crept in, and despite the best analysis, remains open on the system, until maybe, sometime in the future, other information would come to light to downgrade that piece of information or remove it completely.

Unfortunately, sometimes, this never happened and so *corrupted data* would remain on the system. With time, it would gain credibility, the erroneous data corroborating inaccurate data, and in doing so, giving it a veneer of credibility.

The silent mantra of the intelligence community is '*If you can't disprove it, don't discount it*', an infuriating and fucking tough paradox by which to work.

So sadly, on occasions, inaccurate material held on intelligence databases on either side of the pond, combined with coincidence or just bad timing had led to misinterpretations. It had forced Mallory to make very hard decisions.

Sometimes, he made the right choice and other times, tough choices were wrong. On other occasions, Mallory had held back to see, how the game was played out and in doing so, had spared the life of an innocent.

Mallory held the sanctity of life in high regard, but the objective of the operation remained paramount and so, regrettably mistakes had been made.

When a decision was reached, whereby a target (referring to the intelligence patois used to describe the person identified as a compromise) was to be taken out, the sharp-end work was placed in the hands of *wet teams*.

These officially sanctioned assassinations, were by agreement, carried out by personnel from the United Kingdom Special Forces, either SAS (Special Air Service) or SBS (Special Boat Service) both highly trained and unquestionably the most professional SF outfits in the world.

Otherwise, if necessary, and where appropriate, lives were terminated by disinformation given to terrorist or other paramilitary or criminal organisations aimed at encouraging them to plan their own assassination of the target and were designed to actively encourage them into believing that the target was an important capitalist agent or police informant or a catholic or a protestant, Moslem or Jew.

It didn't matter just as long as the target was swiftly dealt with. Too much was at stake.

Each *job* was itself the product of an intricate game designed to give the killing a fireproof history, which would be sufficient to withstand scrutiny by the authorities or the internal intelligence wing of whatever organisation had been manoeuvred into carrying out the act.

The operations once handed over to the British SF were carried out quickly and efficiently and were as humane as possible, in terms of bringing about the end of life.

The other organisations were not as concerned about the niceties of the ethos of quick and clean and usually resorted to interrogation by torture using the most grotesque methods of savagery at the hands of enthusiastic psychopaths.

Invariably, the poor sod on the receiving end would have confessed to the IRA of having shagged the Pope if it could have meant a quick bullet to the head to end it all, instead of another blowtorch session on the bollocks.

The responsibility weighed heavily on the conscience of the custodian, but unfortunately, these methods had to be employed to protect the operation and be in keeping with the professional profile and character of the target in terms of the likely fraternity he or she might have encountered in the past and successfully operated against and inevitably offended. The finger of blame could easily be pointed in the appropriate direction.

To date, the targets eliminated had been considered *peripheral compromises* and all but a few had been from the security services who being intelligent people, by and large, had identified a part of the operation (to no great extent) and in doing so had signed their own death warrants.

The two had been lucky enough to have been recruited to work with Mallory but for the other 16, fortune, lady luck, call it what you will had not been smiling upon them. The business was brutally harsh, but the price of compromise was unimaginable; to date, the integrity of the operation remained watertight and on course.

Mallory leant back in his chair and placed his feet on the right-hand corner of the desk, careful not to scuff the sumptuous green leather surface or the dark walnut surround. The desk, had it been able to talk, would have been able to tell an interesting tale from as far back as the war and the beginning of all of this.

He lifted the mug of steaming hazelnut ground coffee from his blotter and blew the steam away before taking the first sip. As he did so, he glanced at the file on his lap and then. moved slightly replacing the mug back onto the blotter. The leather armchair creaked as he moved.

In this age of technology, he was still reluctant to entrust operational material into the binary world of computers because as his own team had shown, any computer or database could be cracked, it just took time, a powerful multi-million-pound Cray computer and the office anorak to patiently carry out the work.

Mallory had all of these at his disposal, which reflected, just how untouchable his department really was.

The team was small and consisted of Mallory, Ryan and Grant. He sometimes joked that it sounded like a bunch of doddery old solicitors. It was doubtful though whether a bunch of solicitors would have the same clout as Mallory's mob.

Mallory's predecessor Mary Forrester had poached him from the security services only three years after leaving Oxford University where he had read law gaining a 1.1 in the process.

He was a gifted scholar and possessed a near-photographic memory. During his brief sojourn with *Box* (the security services) who had recruited him whilst at university, he had become a specialist in intelligence gathering operations. Also, he gained a reputation as a quick analytic learner with a gifted ability to possess a detailed overview of a project and a dozen ways in which to make it work.

Chapter 7
Corporate Trading International

Mallory glanced at his watch, it was nearly 8:45 in the morning, and the ritual of the early morning office meeting would shortly take place at 9 o'clock. This was an opportunity for each member of the team to brief their colleagues on whatever aspect of *The Job* (as it has become known between them) they were involved in.

It was also the opportunity for Mallory to maintain a personal grip on the team and sniff out any quiet issues that might be emerging, whether between his team or within the wider operational community in the UK or USA.

The atmosphere of the meetings was relaxed; affairs and rank were not an issue. Their unique and common bond drew them together almost like a family with Mallory as the father figure. Respect was the datum by which they measured each other, and none were found to be lacking.

At the same time, Grant was entering the secure underground car park used exclusively by Corporate Trading International; the cover company that was essential in legitimising the activities of the few who worked from the building.

The building was a solidly built affair, designed and constructed in 1974, for the sole purpose of *The Job*. It was one of the first buildings in the London docklands to boast an underground car park at a time when the docklands were still a living, breathing industrial area and not the swathe of high-end apartments that evolved out of the old warehouses themselves.

Its location close to St Katherine's dock made it a pleasant area to work, and most importantly, it looked anonymous and inoffensive. Anyone trying to illegally enter the building, would soon come to appreciate that it was a kid leather glove covering an iron fist.

No windows or other apertures were evident on the landside of the building. The only point of entry was the automated high-security entrance into the underground car park and an innocuous-looking door, which served as the delivery point for the mail. A simple brass company nameplate was the only indication of occupancy.

The first floor above the car park, housed the Cray computer, which was protected within an anti-static chamber accessed via an airlock. The purpose of this was to prevent the possibility of any electronic emissions being scanned externally by a *Tempest* capability.

Tempest was and still is a means of remotely mopping up any electronic emissions that are released by a computer without the need for any form of physical device connected to the computer or its associated cables or phone lines. A truly awesome piece of technology that has been around since the era of President Kennedy.

The buildings in the surrounding block had all been purchased by Her Majesty's government through a deniable route and were now owned by several bona fide companies and leased to numerous tenant companies.

The trading, banking, correspondence, administration and associated paraphernalia for Corporate Trading International were controlled by a sophisticated software program that linked all the fictitious strands and wove them into a thoroughly convincing tapestry of normality.

The cover also extended to mail deliveries, telecom providers, insurance, tax forms, national insurance records, local council records and any other public utilities service that may have dealings with a business in the area. On paper or on computer, the building was a bona fide business house with all the necessary correspondence, trivia and bureaucracy expected.

The remaining two floors housed the operations room, which was directly above the computer floor and the general office area occupied the top floor. This was the only floor, which had windows, and these overlooked the Thames itself.

Three standard-looking commercial satellite dishes sat on the roof at different angles, powered by the building's stand-alone power supply. The building had no external power source that could be used as a conduit to eavesdrop on the goings on within.

Another building close by drew power from the national grid that would simulate the same usage as that which would be expected from a building of its size in order to enhance the cover story. The surrogate building to all intents and purposes as far as the national grid was concerned was Corporate Trading International.

For general communications with a small nucleus of other agencies, the de-facto link was by encrypted BRENT 2 phones using a secure ISDN link. Any lengthy communications across the globe, which in the real world would have been carried out by telephone, e-mail or in the past fax, was done using agile-frequency radio transmissions.

Also, for communications with ground teams, *burst data* satellite transmissions were used. The latter method condensed the information into a millisecond transmission that was impossible to detect.

Jayne Grant pulled into her designated parking space and eased herself out of the driver's seat of her Porsche 911 Turbo S Cabriolet. At 28, she was the youngest of the team, petite, blonde and a natural athlete. She attracted more than a casual glance at the wheel of her sports car.

In keeping with the building's cover story, she was dressed in a well-fitted, smart but chic, charcoal grey matching pinstripe jacket and skirt. Grant pressed the fob on the key and the car emitted a sound not unlike the ping of a sonar and all four indicators flashed twice. All was well; the car was locked, which was totally unnecessary really, all things considered.

She placed the fob into her expensive tan leather Christian Dior briefcase that hung like a satchel from her shoulder by a strap. Her heels clipped on the concrete floor as she made her way to the stairs, never the lift in her case, and up to the third floor.

As Jayne entered the office, Tom Ryan was already at his desk. Tom was a dapper chap with a rapier wit who despite wearing a well-tailored Saville Row suit could not hide his athletic and muscular physique, Jayne quietly and guiltily observed, suppressing the rush of a crush.

Tom's hair was a number 1 at the back and sides and finger brushed to the left which combined with his natural tanned complexion and blue/grey eyes made him a quiet magnet for female attention. Although 35, he kept himself fit, more of a weight trainer than a cardiovascular man. Although through his military record showed he was used to the extreme of physical endurance having served as an officer in the SBS.

"Hi, Tom," she said lightly.

"Hello, gorgeous. I'm making a brew; do you fancy one?"

"Black or white today?"

"Black and strong."

"Just like y'men, eh?" he said as he made his way to the coffee pot.

He returned a minute later with a coffee for Jayne and placed it on her desk.

"How's the new motor?" he enquired.

"Great, I'm getting more looks in it than in my old MG," Jayne replied with a beaming smile that caused the lines around her eyes to turn her smile into one which would melt the hardest heart.

"Ah, spanner eyes," said Tom.

"What do you mean?" Jayne replied like a lamb to the slaughter.

"I mean," he said, ever so matter-of-factly, "every time you smile like that, you make my nuts go tight."

Jayne had just taken a sip of her coffee and wasn't ready for the reply. In a half choke, she spat the coffee out into her mug and between gasps, chokes and laughing she called Tom a bastard.

Dave Mallory had just walked out of his office to get another coffee, in time, to see the rather unladylike display.

He smiled quizzically at Tom who just shrugged and grinned boyishly. Mallory just shook his head, turned around and retreated into his office.

At 9 o'clock, a rather sheepish Jayne opened the door into Mallory's office, he waved her in and smiled brushing aside any attempt at an explanation.

Mallory's mind raced back to the first time he had met Tom and Jayne. Tom was in the SBS and was tasked with commanding a wet team to neutralise a target. Jayne was the security service liaison officer designated as Mallory's gofer.

Tom and Jayne, during the initial stages of the operational preparation and planning, had been briefed by Mallory.

Mallory was using the cover of a security service troubleshooter acting on the authority of the PM. He described the target as someone who had been socially engineered into a position some years beforehand, to provide the IRA with intelligence which could assist their political and military struggle.

The identification of a sleeper, or deeply concealed spy, was an achievement as they were the hardest to detect.

Mallory briefed Tom and Jayne on the background of the target, and they discussed at length the target's service history and agreed that the most expedient and plausible method of disposal would be a car bomb. The media and whoever could point the finger at either the IRA or Loyalists.

Tom, during a one-hour briefing to Mallory, led him step-by-step through his operational order and explained the methodology and tactics his team would employ. Jayne was present during the briefing, and afterwards, checked on the target's research log on the SIS computer at Vauxhall.

As with the best-laid plans of mice and men, an oversight had resulted in the target's real research log remaining on the computer system when it should have been replaced with a fictitious one called a false flag; designed to lead any subsequent investigation in the desired direction.

Jayne's enquiry was not noticed by Mallory, until he returned from a meeting in Washington, two days later. By this time, the false flag program had replaced the target's real log and Jayne had since viewed the new log and immediately noticed several striking differences, which she immediately reported to Mallory upon his return.

The records of both enquiries were waiting for Mallory as soon as he logged onto his own computer. Jayne had just become a peripheral compromise.

Jayne had only uncovered that the target had made numerous enquiries on a British national, Jamie Carter an ex-serviceman now living in Jersey in the Channel Islands.

There was nothing remarkable about the character and he was someone who was hardly worthy of the attention of a paramilitary organisation. She had a feeling that the real reason for the operation, however, was on a need-to-know basis and she was being fed disinformation, which she accepted as an operational necessity.

Jayne discussed the research the target has made on Carter with Tom. Tom was reluctant to raise the issue with Mallory, but the damage was done. He too was now a peripheral compromise. Rather unconventionally and in keeping with Tom's personality, he had a mercurial change of heart and laid the facts on the table to Mallory the next time the three met.

Mallory remembered the moment, looking at the pair of them, as they stood in front of him. Both were honest, good young people dedicated to doing what was right. His forefinger rested between his lips and his thumb stroked the stubble on his chin as he deliberated over their fate.

He knew they were his type of people and he could trust them. So, he told them to sit down and chatted to them about themselves and when he was satisfied, he told them the truth. That was five years ago.

"Okay, Boss," said Tom. "Here is y'coffee."

Mallory was shaken from his revere as they took their seats opposite him.

"Thanks, Tom," Mallory said and took a sip of his coffee. "Karl is still on-site and will be back tomorrow."

Karl was Karl Smith not a member of Mallory's *team* or *inner circle* but was a trusted former colleague of Mallory. He could be tasked with difficult and sensitive aspects of the operation without needing to know or more importantly through years of experience, not wanting to know the reason behind any task he was assigned.

Mallory continued, "There is nothing new from the KH-12, it is still providing real-time data to our counterparts in the CIA cell at Langley as well as ourselves."

"Karl is doing a site visit to ensure that the equipment is functional on-site and to verify the integrity of the hardware. It is also an opportunity for him to assess whether there is any possible eventuality that we have overlooked."

"Karl has confirmed that the area is now considered to be a forgotten piece of land and is not used at all by the public due to its inaccessibility caused by the brambles that have grown over time."

"All I can say is that stuff made my life hell in Royal Marines and then later in the SBS when we had to conduct close target reconnaissance or build a covert rural observation post. Trying to get to the area to conduct your CTR or to get to the chosen site of your OP was almost impossible if the area was brambled. That said, once in you were virtually impossible to detect."

Mallory nodded. "Well the good news is that Carter can still get into the area thanks to himself and his dog Fizz, having over time trampled a path through the stuff. Satellite confirms that no one else uses that area apart from those two."

"Boss," said Tom, "I've got to ask, what is Carter's mental state at the moment since he lost his wife in that car crash in February?"

"Intelligence indicates that he has taken it very hard. He drinks himself to sleep, his work is being affected because he always has a hangover, his behaviour is on occasion irrational and he is short-tempered. He is grieving and doesn't give a damn and he is losing it."

"But apart from that he is solid as a rock," Tom said flatly.

"No offence, Boss. But this guy is the centrepiece on a very elaborate stage. If he is so screwed up that he becomes unreliable in my book that makes him a liability. We should adopt a contingency to negate his role within this operation."

"That is not an option open to us Tom, at the moment." Mallory paused to let the end of the last sentence just hang there to have its effect. "You know the score; we can't alter anything that may have any impact on the way Carter will deal with what lies ahead. The events that are taking their toll on him could very well prove to be the catalyst for determining his thought processes and reactive situation responses. This is shaping him, make no bones about that and this emotional ordeal by fire could be vital."

"When you look at what we can clearly confirm through physical evidence of the present day recovered from the past there is no synchronicity. The natural timeline has been broken, whether this is something that can be repaired none of us quite frankly have a clue."

"So, Tom, in answer, of sorts to your observation, we have no option but to go with the intelligence data that we know as fact."

Mallet stood from behind his desk and faced the window looking out over the Thames, lost for a moment in the maelstrom of paradoxes. He breathed out slowly as Tom and Jayne watched this brilliant and highly intelligent man try to intellectually rationalise the words he had just spoken.

Mallory turned and stroked his trimmed goatee beard. "Tom, what Carter experienced was horrific. I'm not sure what I say will make any difference, but you should know that these are the facts which will place into context his love, loss and now loneliness."

"Carter was in love with his wife, Callie. They had no children but shared a very close, intimate and caring life together, their emotional *child* was their little dog, Fizz. Life was perfect. Then one day, Callie remembered a birthday gift that she had bought for one of the new accountants in her business."

"She liked the girl and wanted to make her feel at home, but she had forgotten to leave the present on her desk when she left the evening before, knowing that she would be taking the following day off."

"Despite the protestations of Carter, Callie insisted that she quickly go to work before anyone arrive and pop the present on the desk. Callie promised to be only five minutes and she left smiling with a wave. Carter never saw her again."

"So, what happened, Boss?" Jayne said.

"Well, Callie set out to work in her car, driving down a road called Le Mont Les Vaux. As she took the sweeping right bend, a lorry was heading up the hill carrying plastic drainpipes resting on a bar above the driver's cab. The driver was late and was by all accounts going too fast as he entered the bend."

"The pipes pushed against the poorly tied rope which gave way. The pipes rolled off the bar and through the windscreen of Callie's car. Her death was instantaneous. The aftermath was horrific."

Jayne turned away. "Oh my God, the poor lady. No wonder Carter is so messed up."

Tom stared thoughtfully into his coffee and closed his eyes and said, "Poor bugger…no wonder the bloke is having a breakdown."

"If we knew that, deep down, he still was the soldier that he once was, who is disciplined and focussed, then I would be more optimistic. He is, as we know, understandably a grieving mess."

"I can't quite believe, I'm saying this and I'm not trying to evoke pathos Boss, but Carter could be a danger to the very future of mankind by not giving a fuck and telling all, compromising the D-Day landings and ultimately the defeat of the Allies."

"I agree too," Jayne said, thoughtfully. "The danger is we don't know how Carter will react. What is so unique about him?"

"We just don't know," replied Mallory. "So, all we can do is let nature take its course because it's the only option open to us. Carter is unfortunately just with us for the ride. If we knew more, we could perhaps, approach this situation without him, but we don't and that I fear is what we are left with—no options. Picking up on what Jayne said the main problem is you don't know what you don't know."

"The concerns you are expressing are the ones which have been aired at a much higher level." He uncrossed his legs and leant forward, carefully placing the pen down on his blotter. "The bottom line is, we are acting within a very specific framework. The only latitude we will have is that once the event occurs, options may open up and steer our strategy."

"We have been entrusted with the hefty responsibility of calling the shots on the ground once the operation starts. No second-guessing, that I promise."

"Today, I will be in meetings with SIS and Box and the PM, and then, on Monday lunchtime, I will be flying to Washington for a final meeting with the US agencies."

(To many the term SIS meant nothing and nor did Box. But if you had ever jumped down the rabbit hole the acronyms were clear: Secret Intelligence Service (MI6) and Box (MI5), the latter stands for the old post office mailing address for MI5, Box 500).

"Tom, I want you to prepare a final briefing two days after I return. The operational order can be completed in the final week before deployment. I want the Op. Order to be a solid proposal, something you can hang your hat on."

That signalled the end of the meeting and Tom and Jayne left Mallory's office and returned to their desks.

"Jayne," said Tom.

"What?" she replied.

"I've got something solid that you can hang your hat on any time you fancy."

"Pervert!" she laughed and deftly lobbed a piece of blue tack at him, which, with years of expensive government training, he failed to dodge as it connected with his imaginary hat stand.

Chapter 8
Downing Street

The Daimler swung through the gates of Downing Street shortly after 2 o'clock and glided to a smooth halt outside Number 10. Mallory hopped out of the car and briskly walked into the world's most famous terraced house greeted by a respectful nod from the bobby at the door.

In keeping with Mallory's personality, even this visit was the subject of disinformation to staff and the press. The latter, religiously waited outside like eager puppies hoping for a few scraps off the table. Mallory was for all intents and purposes purporting to be one of those faceless Whitehall mandarins attending a bland but important meeting on farm subsidies.

Mallory made his way to the *tank*, a basement room, which was used for the most secret of secret cabinet and government business. The PM was already there, seated in a sumptuous leather armchair, which formed one of a circle of six such chairs.

"Hello, David," the PM said, standing to shake Mallory's hand.

"Thanks, John. I'm sorry, about all the cloak-and-dagger stuff, but I think, by the time I have explained everything to you, you will understand my caution."

"No need to give excuses, I know you from old. Even at school, you were always the dark horse. My diary is clear for the rest of the afternoon, and if necessary, I can cancel the cocktail party this evening, it's only for the usual party suspects. Please, take a seat."

"I appreciate that very much," Mallory replied sincerely.

He had always liked and respected John whom he considered to be a genuine honest man, a rare breed in a politician; and modest too, which was even rarer.

"John. What I am about to tell you is beyond Top Secret. It is, in fact, so sensitive that any compromise of the information I am about to tell you has been resolved through extreme measures."

Mallory paused to allow his words to take effect. He saw the PM blink slowly and nod for him to continue.

"In 1946, documentation and items were recovered in Berlin that were being smuggled out from the British sector where they had been stored in a building that was formerly the Headquarters of the *Waffen SS*. You can imagine what must have taken place in that hell hole of sadistic Nazi depravation."

"Anyhow, the package shall we call it, was returned to London for examination amidst the tightest security. What transpired was amazing and virtually unbelievable."

The PM shifted in his chair, the anticipation plain to see on his face. "Go on," he said trying not to let the excitement show on his face.

"The documentation and items related to a British national born in Jersey who was detained by the German army of occupation on 15 May 1944. The person was one Jamie Carter."

"What is so out of the ordinary with that? I understand that the Islanders suffered terribly at the hands of the Germans, and if I remember my history correctly, some two thousand were deported to concentration camps in Poland and Germany. Many never returned."

"That's exactly correct, John. But what makes this extraordinary is that, Carter was born after the war and we can confirm this."

Mallory's words hung in the air. The PM leant forward in his chair with his mouth open in astonishment. Mallory just stared at the PM, judging that the leader of His Majesty's government would need a few seconds to collect his thoughts.

"Are you sure? I mean could there have been some sort of mistake in the translation? Is it possible that somehow—" the words faded as the PM forced his mind to slow down.

"I can tell you, John, categorically, this was no mistake. The documentation included photographs of Carter, his driving licence, several bank credit cards, cash, change, clothing, his Rolex and a Nokia mobile phone. The Germans were just as flabbergasted by this as we were."

"So, what happened to Carter?"

"We don't know. The building housing the Headquarters of the Waffen SS was destroyed. What I can confirm is that Carter is alive and well and living in Jersey."

The PM sat back heavily into his chair and removed his glasses, absentmindedly chewing on one arm of the glasses as he stared at the figurine on the mantelpiece.

"So, what do we know about Carter?" he asked, still staring at the bronze sculpture of the pirouetting ballerina.

"Carter joined the Royal Marines and after training he was posted to four-five commando. He remained in service for 12 years, the majority of which he spent in the SBS having passed selection at the age of 22. He was a qualified marksman and was, and still remains a freefall parachutist. He was married but his wife died in February of this year."

"When he left the SBS, he joined his father's offshore business in Jersey and made a packet dealing in stocks. The downside is that he has taken the loss of his wife badly. He is drinking heavily and has become somewhat unreliable."

"He doesn't need to work but still dabbles in the futures market, and recently, made a massive venture capital investment in a Silicon Valley outfit called Solaris Industries, which has become globally huge. He is worth millions."

"He remains fit despite his drinking and an assessment is that his level of fitness is easily that of an SF trooper. He runs five miles a day, even with a hangover, and doesn't let up even after puking. Also, he religiously spends 90 minutes in the gym each day. He also does the mixed martial arts, which is the most impressive form of fighting; deadly and brutal."

"What initiatives are in place regarding Mr Carter?" the PM asked.

"Needless to say," Mallory began, "Carter's cottage has been entered and intrusive devices have been placed to record audio and visual intelligence. The product is simultaneously relayed to CESG, the old GCHQ at Cheltenham, and to the NSA to ensure that nothing is overlooked."

"Are CESG and the National Security Agency swapping the same notes?" the PM asked.

Mallory admired the former barrister for his ability to see the lateral side of an *event*.

"I can assure you that they are, Sir. The NSA holds CESG in high regard and vice-versa. There is a free flow of information and both agencies are far too professional to be anything other than the best of friends."

"To be quite frank, they know that the likes of you and I will come and go, whereas they will remain the same, a datum. I find that quite reassuring."

"Anyhow, based on the recovered documentation, we know the exact area where Carter was apprehended by the Wehrmacht. As a result of this, a KH-12 satellite was commissioned specifically for the operation, and was launched in March this year from Vandenberg AFB, and is now in a geostationary orbit 322 kilometres above Jersey."

Mallory continued, "A full reconnaissance of the area, which incidentally is called Noirmont," the PM interrupted, "Black Mount, a bit bleak and unfriendly sounding, I must say."

"Quite," Mallory replied, before continuing. "As I said, the area has been fully reconnoitred and geo-sensors have been dug in to provide a remote surveillance capability to determine what traffic, for want of a better word, there is on the headland. The geo-sensors can determine the difference between a human footfall to that of an animal."

"Why is that important?" the PM interjected.

"Because we will need to know exactly where anything and everything is, which could possibly have any bearing on what is going to take place. Additionally, other seismic devices have been deployed along with specialist sensors capable of detecting variations in the normal physics of the area."

"The KH-12 satellite is a hybrid piece of technology that is equipped with an array of monitoring hardware that will be able to detect any shifts in the Earth's electromagnetic field along with the slightest plate-tectonic or seismic activity."

The PM looked puzzled and said, "I thought that technology was still under development between Stanford University and NASA, and wouldn't be achievable for at least 18 months?"

Mallory smiled. "Officially, that's correct. Unofficially, it's been up there for about a month. John, you do realise the possible impact of Carter's capture. We are talking about an individual who would have grown up having been taught at school the history of the Second World War."

"Most importantly, they would have in their hands, an individual who would know not only the date of the invasion of Normandy but also, the exact landing sites and they would have more than enough time to organise their defences before 6 June. The entire outcome of the war could change and with it the history as we know it."

Chapter 9
Leaving Downing Street

Mallory sat back into the soft cream leather of the Daimler. He had been with the PM for just over five hours running through the proposed *modus operandi* for next week, the 25th. So much could go wrong. His greatest fear was that they would be unable to recreate the environment that *would* take Carter into enemy territory and possibly to his death.

Mallory reflected on how the PM had uncomfortably raised the issue of *neutralising* Carter before the event. This was the proverbial old chestnut that had been mooted on many occasions, only to be rebuffed on the grounds of better the devil you know.

It was quite conceivable that if Carter was taken out of the frame, some other unfortunate and unknown individual could inadvertently take his place. The consensus had always erred on the side of caution, if there was such a thing under the circumstances.

Mallory looked out of the window and remembered Tom's earlier comment as the car sped through the drizzle of a typical dark and dreary London evening. Thinking, *if only we knew more, but then again, you don't know what you don't know.*

The Daimler dipped down the ramp and into the basement of *Corporate Trading International*. The security gates smoothly closed as the car eased to a halt outside of the executive lift.

Mallory thanked the driver, a fully *badged* member of the SBS from Tom's old troop who was on secondment to the unit. Mallory decided to give the lift a miss, taking the stairs to the third floor.

As he entered the office, Tom was pouring over the latest imagery from the KH-12 as he made the final adjustments to the planning.

"Hello, Boss. Fancy a coffee?"

"Why not, the night is young. Where's Jayne?"

"Out doing something girly and meaningless, I suppose. Should never have given them the vote," Tom mumbled as he bent over his desk looking at the latest *takes*.

"I love your banter, Tom, and I can't wait until Jayne is your boss!" Mallory said trying to make Tom bite the hook.

Tom just returned Mallory the same boyish grin as this morning.

Mallory laughed and said, "More importantly, do you want something with that coffee you're going to make me?"

"Bushmills?" Tom asked hopefully, raising an eyebrow.

"Got it in one," was the reply.

A couple of minutes later, they were both sitting in the main office, with their feet resting on desks as they sat back in their chairs.

"So, how is the planning going, Tom?" Mallory asked as he sipped the hot coffee, enjoying and inhaling the hot whisky and coffee vapour.

"Fine, fairly straightforward up until Carter slips into the ether. Basically, the area will be covered by our friendly KH-12 and will cover Carter's approach route from his home address and to the estimated point, where the event will take place."

"There will be a four-man team in close proximity to follow the subject through to wherever."

"How do you propose to return?"

"I don't know," Tom replied honestly. "I'm going to have to rely on you chaps for that. Just as long as we can keep Carter in our control, and get him back across as soon as possible and not lose him into enemy hands I will be happy."

"What if?" Mallory asked, posing the type of question that made Tom groan inwardly. "You don't get across or he falls into enemy hands?"

"Would we ever know? If Carter was captured and revealed everything under interrogation. We would have no comprehension of what had taken place seconds earlier the event occurred and he disappeared into the night?"

"What is the composition of your team?" Mallory asked.

"I am the ground team Operational Commander and explosives guru. Austin Grey was *Mr Nasty* on my SBS selection course, then later, one of my squadron sergeants. I have made him my deputy ground commander. He is also a sniper, a trained medic to combat medic standards and the best comms man I know."

"The other two lads are Sergeant Nick Bennet. Bennet is a highly professional climber and climbed Everest as part of the British expedition three years ago. He is an explosives man too and an Arab, German and French linguist. He speaks

French with a Parisian accent and German with a Berlin accent."

"Both he and I are the weaker linguists, but we would still pass as a local in either language. The other lad is Sergeant Jim Stevenson; another explosives man, French and German linguist and resident judo expert who represented England at the last Olympics. They are all very, very hard bastards."

"Additionally, Boss, all four of us have recently been to the Foreign Office Language School and received the Foreign Office thumbs up for our French and German," Tom added.

Mallory smiled looking over the brim of his mug and asked, "Why have you chosen all SBS troopers, instead of SAS?"

"To be honest, it's a case of trust. An awful lot depends on this mission, and I would prefer to have guys that I have worked with. In these circumstances, trust is earned from having worked together in real life or in intense-scenario training exercises like taking a North Sea oil rig back from terrorists."

"Believe me, we fin away from a submarine, then swim to the target in our re-breathers, assault kit and comms. Then, climb another 100 feet up the legs of the rig in gale force seas and then successfully attack and re-capture the structure, you need a team that works like clockwork. These are my boys, and we work well together."

Mallory leant forward placing the now half-full cup on the desk, looked at Tom square in the eye and said, "I need you to provide me with a complete list of all the equipment you propose to take. I want you to travel as light as you can but still have the combined firepower to overwhelm and annihilate any opposition you encounter."

Mallory paused. "Tom, I need to know your contingencies for the disposal of any of your team that are taken down. Every trace, and I mean every trace of the body and unusable equipment will need to be destroyed. By that, I mean, vaporised by an explosion. We can't get sentimental about this operation until it is over."

Mallory held the cup in his hand and made slow circles on the coaster, causing the contents to steam and swirl around the inner walls of the surface.

Tom replied, "The team have been there before, and we all know what is at stake. The boys know and we accept the odds are against us. We are prepared to do what is asked of us."

Tom looked out of the window and back in his mind's eye to an operation in the Eastern bloc as it was then several years before.

"I can tell you this much, Boss, the four of us were on an Op where we had to leave mates behind who had been killed. We left no trace of them. When we sleep we all have nights in the dark lands where the memories come back to haunt us. But you deal with it and remember your mates with fondness over a beer."

Mallory looked at Tom as he continued to gaze at the window and into his past, "That's why I know, my team will do what's right because we've done it before. They're a good bunch, Boss, we won't let you down."

Mallory placed his hand on Tom's shoulder as he quietly left. The door gently clicked as it closed. His mind was a maelstrom of activity, processing scenario after scenario, contemplating how the mission could play out.

As he reached the underground car park of Corporate Trading International, he pulled the keys to his Porsche Macan from his jacket pocket. With his finger in the metal ring, he swung the keys into his palm and then, activated the car's anti-theft device on the black fob.

The quality precision engineering of the central locking system was personified by the muted clunk of the doors as the locking mechanism was released. There was no accompanying ping or flash of indicators or other suggestions that anything had taken place. It was just a mellow and subtle sound of class. The car was very much a mirror of its owner.

Mallory opened the driver's door and was greeted by the sumptuous smell of leather and polished walnut. A turn of the key in the ignition and the beast began to purr. Mallory pulled out of his space and through the security gates which were automatically linked to an encrypted device within the vehicle.

It negating the need for a manually operated one which could be lost and potentially compromise the security of the building. Each vehicle that was parked in the underground complex was fitted with the same device. The purr became a growl as Mallory accelerated into the damp cold night.

Chapter 10
Scumbag Alley

Tom heard the click of the door as the boss left. He slowly walked out of his cloud of thoughts and heard his mobile come alive to the sound of Hot Chocolate's *You sexy thing*. The ringtone belonged to Jayne's number.

Tom smiled to himself, his spirits lifting as he answered, "Hi, Gorgeous."

Jayne smiled, replying, "I'm at that new wine bar just around the corner from the office, it's called Giovanni's. Fancy popping along and buying me a glass or two of bubbles?"

"Giovanni's?" Tom replied, thinking where it might be. "Ah yes, I know the one full of bankers," passing on the obvious pun.

"That's the one. It's nice! Better than that old spit and sawdust dockers pub, be here in 15 minutes. I fancy a couple of glasses, so I've left my car at work. I'll pick it up tomorrow."

"Sounds like a plan. I'll leave the old banger here too. See you soon, bye."

Tom swung his feet off the desk and cleared the papers and imagery away, securing them in his personal safe.

Mallory was fastidious that everyone maintained a clear desk policy even in such a highly secure place as CTI. It was just another indication of the team's collective professionalism. They didn't allow themselves to fall into a comfort zone created by the building's security, whereby bad practices and sloppy procedures would become the norm.

Subconsciously, Tom swept the room to check that it was sterile, that it was free from any operational material. It was.

Satisfied, he picked up his jacket from the back of his chair and slid the garment on, pulling on both lapels to straighten the weight and drop off the fabric across his shoulders. The fine cut of the Italian silk served to enhance his chiselled physique beneath.

Tom left the building and turned right into the damp night walking the quarter of a mile to the new bar. He passed several properties that were under renovation and some recently refurbished warehouses that were now on the market.

He had looked at the estate agent brochures on a couple of the apartments (the term *flat* was now considered passé) and was quite taken with one in particular.

Once the next few weeks were out of the way, he was going to make a determined effort to put some roots down and get his own place instead of renting, albeit a cracking apartment, which was just dead money at the end of the day.

He took a shortcut through a narrow lane, glistening in the evening damp and occasional drizzle and passed several black cabs that were always parked waiting to collect punters from the several restaurants and pubs nearby.

Tom turned left, past a boarded and derelict building. The sign said that it was due to be demolished to make way for more luxury apartments. He then turned right and back into the main drag, emerging back into the streetlights of civilisation and the welcoming sight of Giovanni's.

Den and Lee were sitting in the Red Lion geographically, just around the corner from Giovanni's but a world away in terms of class. The pub's clientele were prostitutes, druggies (or both) or small-time crooks who thought they were big-time hard cases. Lager was the drink of choice and tattoos were much in evidence, even some of the blokes had them.

Lee had spent the past few minutes making none-too-subtle small talk with a prostitute called Josie. She let him grab her arse as she thought she was on her way to making a few notes for five minutes of work in the toilets. Lee didn't want to pay, and Josie told him to fuck off.

He was going to give the slag a slap when Den tugged the back of Lee's football shirt to let him know that a big lard arse called Rigger (who was the tarts pimp) was currently drilling Lee with his coal-black eyes. He hoped something would kick off and he could beat the shit out of Lee and slice his face open.

Lee knew Rigger's reputation and settled for telling Josie to fuck off. Honour demanded that he didn't back down too much. So, he ordered another couple of lagers and a pack of dry-roasted nuts for him and Den.

Lee and Den had known each other since Borstal nearly 20 years ago. Now in their late 30s, they had spent a life of crime together and had both done a fair bit of time inside. It was nothing compared to the crime and misery they had caused but never been arrested or convicted of.

They both had begun their lives of crime stealing cars and mugging those they knew were easy targets, typically pensioners. Those who were smaller and more vulnerable than they were, and even, on occasions, someone in a wheelchair.

It was a laugh. They needed the money for drugs and drink and these fucking weak tossers could spare the dosh. They took pleasure in humiliating their victims; they pissed all over one old wanker in a wheelchair and taunted the husband of a pensioner that he was too old to fucking look after his wife before indecently assaulting her in front of him.

Had they known the consequences of their actions and had they been bothered to read the papers, they would have known that a week after the attack, the elderly wife took an overdose. She was too ashamed of what had taken place in front of her beloved husband.

A week after her passing and wracked with guilt at his inability to protect his dear wife and sickened at his cowardice in not trying to defend her (difficult to do if you're crippled with arthritis and walk with two sticks), he committed suicide by hanging himself in the garden shed.

He was found a few days later by his daughter, still clutching the wedding photo in his death grip. As such the ripple effect continued.

Lee had increasingly become more sexually focussed when he chose to humiliate a victim. A few months back, they had mugged a German exchange student who was making her way through the park just after teatime. She felt safe; it was early, and the streetlights were on and shining on the pavement brightly on the other side of the park railings.

Lee and Den had been in the pub for the afternoon and had lost some money on the horses and were now short and needed some lolly for a score and some booze. They saw the girl approach, head down with a rucksack over her shoulder clasping her folders against her chest.

Lee had asked her for a light, and she tried to walk past him. The fucking bitch was ignoring him so he grabbed her, and she struggled dropping her folders. At the same time, he saw her shirt had become unbuttoned and he could see her bra beneath.

He could feel himself becoming aroused and pushed her to the ground. Den checked around, there was nobody else in view. He held her down as Lee undid his belt and dropped his fake Armani's. The girl was beyond fear and was sobbing. This just served to turn Lee on more, he was in total control.

Lee wasn't gentle he just enjoyed himself. When she screamed, he punched her to keep her quiet. When he was done, Den took over, he didn't give a fuck about sloppy seconds; the bitch had a fit body. In the real world, he would never have had the chance with a girl as good-looking as her, so he made the most of it.

When they were done, Lee gave the bitch a kick in the guts and told her they would fucking kill her if she grassed to the pigs. The girl remained motionless, too terrified to move. In total fear, she had lost bowel and bladder control, and now, lay in her own mess. The feeling of violation was too enormous to comprehend.

She lay crumpled on the edge of the path for what seemed a lifetime before a passing uniformed police patrol saw a figure through the railings. In minutes, an ambulance was en route and the physical wounds would be tended to and the compassionate but clinical post-rape process would begin. The mental scars would take years to heal.

In all from the time of the rape to the arrival of the ambulance, a mere life-changing 40 minutes had elapsed. Lee and Den were still pissed off, they still didn't have the money for their next fix and after all that exercise, they could murder a beer.

As Tom entered Giovanni's, he was engulfed by the smell of expensive women in cheap perfume or something like that. This was the sort of place where people judged the person standing next to them by the quality of a fashion label or the name on their watch.

Tom had already been approved by some of the female clientele who saw the Nino Cerruti label on the inside of his jacket as he raised his arm to wave at Jayne, and at the same time exposed his Rolex submariner.

Jayne was sitting away from the main bar in a snug area filled with expensive, comfy leather armchairs in a pseudo fireside library setting. Jayne's choice of armchairs offered a well-positioned but discreet view of the rest of the wine bar. A good choice to sit if you enjoy the sport of people-watching.

Jayne returned Tom's wave by raising her glass of bubbles followed by a top-end Shiraz, knowing that he was a red wine man. As Tom approached, he peeled himself out of his jacket, much to the enjoyment of several females who admired the athletic way in which he did this, whilst pondering the toned and muscular body that lay beneath.

One of them handed Tom a glass of Shiraz.

"Thanks, Jayne," he replied oblivious to the glances he was getting.

Jayne liked the way in which Tom was unaware of just how attractive he was. He was almost boyish in his innocence which made him even more appealing. Despite the quips, witty comments and sexual innuendo in the office, Jayne knew it was all a front to cover his shyness around her.

The pair chatted easily. Tom subconsciously was psychologically safe in the knowledge that they were work colleagues having a sociable drink after a hard week. He had liked Jayne from the moment he first met her. But he found her a bit awkward to be around because she was so intense and sometimes, he could never decipher the tone in her voice. It was easier to be the clown than to start peeling back the onion and let anyone in.

The sport of people-watching is one common amongst those in the intelligence business who spend a significant amount of their time interpreting the actions of others from a distance; either by way of surveillance or looking down a camera lens or as in Tom's case a sniper scope. In the innocent theatre of life, the stage changes but the mannerisms of the cast of characters rarely stray from the plot.

As the wine flowed, Tom passed comments over several punters. One self-indulgent woman, decked out in expensive Channel, in Tom's opinion had a face like a bag of spanners, which when she spoke, looked none too dissimilar to a bulldog chewing a wasp.

Jayne frequently was caught off-guard by Tom's dry and sometimes, coarse observations; the product of a Royal Marine and SBS career. It surfaced out of nowhere and with little warning, causing Jayne on a couple of occasions to cover her mouth and nose as the champagne went in one way and came down another.

It was Jayne's turn to get the wine. Tom admired the sensual sway of her hips as she glided to the bar. Two of the barflies parted as she approached to give her a space between them.

Jayne grinned and they smiled back, unaware that Jayne was, in fact, smiling at a comment Tom had made earlier; one had a face like a slapped arse and his chubby mate with the big teeth had more chins than a Chinese phone directory.

Tom was slouched in the world's most comfy armchair, with no tie and with the top two buttons of his Jermyn Street shirt undone as he watched Jayne at the bar. He became aware of someone leaning towards him from a chair at his side.

He turned and his eyes followed a long pair of tanned legs. The owner of the legs had her arms crossed over the knees as she leant forward giving Tom's trained sniper eyes a clear shot down her ample cleavage.

The lizard (in the parlance of the military) spoke before Tom had looked at the speaker's face, "I don't know why you waste your time with cheap little tarts like her."

The voice was posh and nasally and carried on it the smell of too many cigarettes. He realised that the Channel suit was talking to him, her cluck of girlie friends were giggling, confident, that he was a sure thing for their irresistible and expensively well-dressed friend.

At that moment, Jayne looked back from the bar and saw the old vulture leaning over Tom as if he was a piece of carrion. A pang of jealousy ran through her, and she was surprised by her reaction.

Tom locked eyes with Jayne and gave her a quick grin and a surreptitious wink before turning back to the ego in the Channel suit and her audience. "Sorry, I didn't realise it was Halloween. I'd be very grateful if you and the other broomstick pilots could Foxtrot Oscar into the night and leave me to enjoy my evening."

Relief swept through Jayne as she watched as the Channel suit and her entourage departed. The suit's face contorted as she spat out a reply to Tom, who amid the torrent, turned back around to Jayne and gave her another beaming boyish grin.

The rest of the evening flew by, and soon, it was that time.

"Are you going to be okay getting home or do you want to share a cab with me?"

Jayne smiled. "It's alright, there's a taxi rank in the next street. I'll get a cab there, anyway, you live miles from me but thanks all the same."

Tom helped Jayne into her charcoal jacket. She turned around and he saw that a strand of her hair had broken free of the scrunch and was dangling loose at the side of her face. He gently pushed it back over her ear, looking deeply into her eyes, afraid to take the next step; the possibility of rejection and all that would entail would be too awkward.

Jayne smoothed the errant piece of hair back and retied the scrunch. "Thanks," she whispered, blushing slightly as she studied her shoes, unknowingly thinking the same as Tom.

"I'll see you on Monday. I really enjoyed tonight, bye." Giving Tom a genuinely happy smile, Jayne turned quickly away and into the throng of the crowded bar.

"Bye, gorgeous," Tom whispered to her back, watching her for as long as he could, before losing her petite form amidst the unwanted crowd.

At about the same time, Lee and Den were finishing up their lagers in the Red Lion and were intending to go to one of the late-night boozers for a few more. The beers were flowing tonight, thanks to a posh twat they had knifed the day before, a few streets down as he got into his Mercedes in one of those private carparks by the docks. The wanker had five hundred notes in his wallet and deserved the kicking he got.

They nicked his car and sold it to a contact Lee had met in the nick who was in the east end ganglands. His ex-prison buddy was very keen to make the deal and took the car in exchange for notes. So, on top of the five hundred big ones they'd robbed, they got another five grand for the motor and a Colt 45. It was a class piece that came with 50 rounds and a spare mag. Fucking awesome.

Like kids with a new toy, they had taken turns to have the gun stuffed down the waistband of their fake designer jeans. Lee decided to keep the spare magazine and the rest of the ammo in the safe stash he had under the kitchen sink floorboards in his gaff but they were now carrying a gun on the street.

They were climbing up the greasy gangland pole and would soon have their own turf and prestige (so, their friend coke told them).

They left the Red Lion and walked past the boarded-up old warehouses waiting to be developed and then into a side street. As they turned the corner Lee saw a petite figure in a charcoal shirt and jacket, walking briskly towards them; her arms were wrapped across her chest to keep warm against the chill of the night.

Jayne had seen the pair turn into the dark and quiet street but she had been halfway down by that stage and unable to avoid having to walk past them. Her senses were screaming at her to get away. Her heart rate started to increase and she looked down to avoid eye contact and quickened her pace, crossing to the opposite side of the road.

Lee nudged Den and nodded towards Jayne as she came nearer on the pavement across from them. Den smiled.

"Oy, love, fancy going to a party?" Lee shouted.

Shit, thought Jayne and ignored them.

Lee crossed over the road blocking her direct path. Den remained on the same side and walked behind Jayne, cutting off any chance of escaping back the way she had just come.

"I'm fucking talking to you, bitch! Don't fucking ignore me!" said Lee and grabbed Jayne by the upper arm as she tried to sidestep him and pushed her against the hoarding of one of the abandoned warehouses, which gave slightly as she fell against it.

Lee leant close to Jaynes's face. She could smell the stale lager, the sweat and the fags on his rancid breath.

"You stuck-up bitches are all the same, think you're too posh for me and my mate," as he spoke, he slid his hand inside Jaynes's jacket.

Lee's face was a matter of inches from her own. Jayne pulled her head back and crashed her forehead into Lee's face, striking him across the nose and his top row of teeth.

Lee recoiled in pain, his nose streaming blood. He swung a punch blindly catching Jayne fully on the right cheekbone. Jayne fell heavily against the hoarding and onto the soaking pavement.

Lee was standing with his legs astride cupping his face in his hands. He kicked the hoarding with such force that it gave way, falling into the abandoned building.

"Den, get the fucking bitch in there," he shouted.

He crouched down beside Jayne who was close to unconsciousness and whispered between blooded, clenched teeth, "You are gonna get taught a fucking lesson for that, you're never going to forget tonight, bitch!"

Tom left Giovanni's and started to walk back towards the office. He had no intention of going into the office, it was just that he wanted to make sure that Jayne had got a taxi safely. He pulled out his mobile and punched in her number. No reply.

Tom stared at his phone. A sense of nausea and worry washed over him making his stomach turn. Jayne and her mobile were inseparable, she would have heard the phone ringing whether she was walking, talking or in a taxi. She never ignored a call, especially, if she recognised the number.

He quickly ran through the possibilities of which taxi rank she might have been heading to. The closest was the one on the way back towards the office, but to get there you had to walk past those derelict buildings.

"Scumbag alley," Tom said quietly to himself and started to run.

As he turned into the dark wet street, he saw figures down the far end. It was too dark to make out exactly what was going on, it could be pissed mates helping an even more pissed mate to get up after tripping over.

Tom closed in quickly and for a second he felt as if his heart had stopped. Two men were manhandling a limp but still struggling form into the old warehouse. The sight of the torn charcoal jacket lying nearby filled him with a rage, which he focussed through years of deadly training.

"Evening wankers," Tom said in a quiet and controlled voice.

Lee and Den spun around shocked that they hadn't heard anyone approach.

Lee straightened up, he felt the grip of the 45 and a sense of control washed over him, almost as cool as the rush of smack or coke. He pulled the 45 out of his waistband and pointed it at Tom.

Den, who was dragging Jayne into the building by her arms, let her go and joined Lee, pulling out his knife and watching the blade glint in the ambient light. The last time he had pulled this little baby out another fucking banker had felt cold steel.

"A bit outgunned tosser," Lee spat. "I'll shoot your fucking dick off, then you can watch me fuck your little slag here."

"Then, I'll do her after, and again, and again. Fucking city prick," laughed Den.

Tom ignored the verbals. The first millisecond was used to make a visual casualty assessment of Jayne. She appeared to have been roughed up but untouched. No life-threatening injuries. A stable casualty.

In the next millisecond, Tom concentrated instead on the weapons and their owner's handling of them. The twat with the gun had Tom in the backsight, but the foresight was at least 30 degrees off to Tom's left.

The icing on the cake was that the safety was still on. This nobber had only ever seen guns on TV, he certainly didn't know jack shit about how to use one.

That left the other prick with the knife. He held it low in his right hand and in a weaving side-to-side motion with his left hand out palm up. Just like in true Hollywood style.

Tom concluded that they had no weapon-handling skills and were street thugs. Training taught him never to underestimate an opponent as luck can just as easily win over skill.

The most immediate threat was the knife. Tom approached Den. Den was unsure what he should do next, he obviously hadn't watched that part of the movie, so he began to make thrusting stabbing motions towards Tom.

"Come on, tosser!" Den shouted, his voice raising a pitch or two.

Tom allowed Den to thrust forward again. This time, he caught Den's right wrist with his right hand as the blade shot past. Using Den's momentum, Tom pulled Den off balance and placed his left hand on Den's right tricep, which was now twisted upwards, then drove the knifeman into the pitted tarmac.

Den's chin hit first causing it to break and smashing his lower set of teeth against the kerbside. Den groaned unable to make any other sound as he had bitten through his tongue.

Tom twisted Den's shoulder to its full natural movement, pulling it up towards him as he crashed down onto the shoulder blade with his left knee dislocating the shoulder and tearing the rotator cuff ligaments apart.

Tom let the arm drop away; the knife was still in Den's puffy and deformed hand. No need to do any more damage, the target was safely out of the game.

Lee watched in horror in the few seconds it had taken Tom to deal with Den, and now, he saw his Nemesis walking towards him. He fumbled with the gun as it shook nervously in his right hand.

"Stay away from me, you fucking tosser, or I'll blow you and the bitch away!" as he spoke, he pointed the gun in the direction of Jayne and then, at Tom, back and forth.

Tom saw that the safety was still on, and a smile began to crease his face as he moved directly towards Lee.

Lee pointed the gun at Tom and squeezed the trigger. It didn't move, nothing happened. He took it off-target and stared at it in disbelief. Then, quickly brought it back up in line with Tom and squeezed the trigger again. The same, nothing happened.

Tom had closed in on Lee and punched him squarely in the sternum, sufficiently away from the solar plexus so as not to shatter it and send fragments into Lee's heart. Tom wanted the jerk to live with his body the way he was about to re-shape it.

Air gushed out of Lee's lungs and he dropped to his knees; the gun falling from his grasp and skittering harmlessly across the puddled road. Lee vomited.

Tom kicked Lee hard in the groin. As Lee rolled over, unable to speak through the fiery agony coursing through his body, his outstretched leg spanned the kerb onto the road. Tom raised his heel and with tremendous force brought it crashing down onto Lee's kneecap.

The patella shattered and the joint tore from the ligaments causing it to bend in the opposite direction to the way nature had intended.

A kick in the cheekbone was sufficient to fracture both it and the jaw as fragmented teeth tore the left side of Lee's tongue to shreds.

Jayne had witnessed her two would-be rapists transformed into lifetime cripples in a mere 15 seconds as Tom, in a controlled fury, dispensed summary justice that went some way to atoning for tonight's crime and the ones they had gotten away with. That said divine retribution would still await them one day.

As Tom crossed to Jayne, she was half standing and half leaning against the hoarding. Her hair was cascading across her face, which was reddening on one side from the punch she had received from Lee.

Tom picked up Jayne's jacket and placed it across her shoulders. He quickly scanned the area to check that they had not left anything behind; satisfied, he began to lead Jayne away.

"Stop!" Jayne said.

Tom did. Jayne walked back to Lee who was vomiting through his broken jaw and smashed teeth. He recoiled as he saw her approach.

Jayne looked down at the whimpering piece of shit and quietly said, "This is for all the other women whose lives you've ruined, you fucking animal!" She kicked Lee with all her strength in his groin with a force and accuracy borne out of indignation and revenge.

Lee had attempted to protect himself but to no avail and only succeeded in having a further four fingers broken as they came between Jayne's kick and his scrotum.

"Nice one!" said Tom, like a commentator at a rugby match, as he, then, ushered Jayne away.

Tom guided Jayne from the street, where she had so nearly been raped and dog legged on several occasions to throw off anyone who may have taken an interest in them.

They found a tiny café called Tony's a mile away and Jayne slipped into the toilet to freshen up, emerging a short time later, looking remarkably together. As they left, the shakes began as the adrenalin began to burn off and Tom hugged Jayne close to him as she began to shudder and sob.

"I really thought it was going to happen. I felt hopeless and so frightened."

"I could tell you'd put up a fight by the injury to the bastard's nose and mouth. You did so well, most other women probably would have been too scared to try," As he said this, Tom held Jayne close until the shaking had stopped.

Jayne looked up at Tom through puffy, tearful eyes and said, "What made you walk down that bloody street, the chances of that happening are so remote."

Tom explained about the unanswered call.

"Oh my God!" exclaimed Jayne, "I remember that happening." She pulled out her mobile and saw an unanswered call.

"Adonis?" Tom said as he peeked at the screen.

Despite everything, Jayne blushed, "It's just a silly name for the phone, in case it gets lost."

Jayne's fingers had suddenly become thumbs as she fumbled to switch the phone in embarrassment and in doing so, didn't see the smile on Tom's lips.

The following morning, Tom phoned Mallory and told him of the previous evening events. Tom had seen Jayne safely home and stayed for a coffee to make sure she was okay, before leaving just after 1 o'clock in the morning.

Mallory agreed with Tom's actions. Based on the way the thugs had been left in the street, it would be assumed that they had been the victims of a turf war confrontation between villains. Mallory resolved to find out through his sources about what had happened to the two attackers and would update Tom on Monday.

Mallory hung up and went to his secure Brent phone and placed a call.

Chapter 11
Vandenberg Space Force Base

Colonel Mike O'Hearn, the mission director was not at his seat in the elevated control desk at the 30th Space Wing. A member of the elite 2nd Space Launch Squadron, he was a senior commander of a unit that formed part of the 30th Space Wing and held sole responsibility for all space lift operations.

The wing was responsible for all Department of Defense space and missile launches, and as this particular payload fell under that umbrella, Vandenberg AFB was its point of departure. The base located at 34.7 degrees north latitude enabled missiles or other space vehicles to be launched due south, without having to pass over the continental USA and all points south until Antarctica.

In addition to the safe splashdown of spent delivery vehicles that harmlessly land in the ocean, the security advantages of polar orbit launches—primarily invisible from land—have made Vandenberg the most discreet launch site for reconnaissance satellites.

Colonel O'Hearn traditionally visited the launch pad on the eve of the scheduled departure His visit although idiosyncratic and essentially unnecessary, formed a part of his good luck ritual for each mission.

In the same way, Gene Kranz had worn a new handmade waistcoat at the launch of every Apollo mission that he was mission director of, Mike O'Hearn felt the need to give the Titan a quick visual once over and a good luck pat on the ass; probably a hangover from his days as a fighter pilot and those pre-flight checks before take-off.

Col O'Hearn swung his M998 cargo/troop-carrying variant of the Humvee onto the hardstand at the base of Launch Pad SLC-4E. The V8 6.2 litre, fuel-injected diesel, liquid-cooled engine had easily propelled the Hummer, down the approach road to the pad at well over the advertised 65 mph. There was still a fighter jock in the Colonel's blood.

SLC stood for Space Launch Complex and the designation 4E simply meant that it was the fourth pad east and was solely used for launching Titan IVBs. Its neighbour across the way SLC-4W was used for Titan II launches.

The Colonel looked up at the 40-storey high concrete gantry that provided all the peripherals necessary to support a launch. Most importantly, keeping the massive billion-dollar launch vehicle safe and secure from the sometimes stormy weather that rolled in from the Pacific and battered the base northwest of Santa Barbara.

In case, anyone was in any doubt as to what purpose the huge concrete structure was for, the uppermost third of the building bore the legend *USAF* with the words *Titan IV* descending down the body of the gantry in the same manner as the iconic lettering on the Apollo rockets.

The Colonel hopped out of the Hummer and rode the access lift to the top of the gantry. Despite the early hour and the slight chill, the air was almost alive with anticipation as the close-down crew conducted their final visual sweep of the launch vehicle, peripherals and structure, ensuring that no last-minute mishap would jinx the launch.

O'Hearn smiled at Lieutenant Spike Andrews, a West Point graduate with a Masters in Chemical Engineering. Outside of the military, Spike could be earning a packet doing research, but instead, he had chosen a career in the military and was one to watch for the future.

Colonel O'Hearn had just completed the endorsement on Lt Andrew's fitness report. The kid was a detail man, well respected by his peers and subordinates and had a laid-back management style, much like O'Hearn's. Like his boss, Andrews got things done.

"Hi, Spike," O'Hearn said raising his hand in greeting.

"Sir, good to see you on this fine March morning," quipped Andrews.

His hands were full of manuals and checklists, but he was still going to attempt a salute.

O'Hearn gave Spike a wave that conveyed *don't worry about that crap* and said, "It's okay, Spike, there are no enlisted ranks here. How is the close-down progressing, what's the status?"

"Sir," began Andrews, "we are confident that the close down will be completed by 05:30 hours, if anything, the team are running ahead of schedule, which means that we can devote a bit of extra time to the foreign object damage sweep."

O'Hearn nodded his agreement, recalling an incident on 18 September 1980 at launcher 374-7 at Little Rock AFB in Arkansas when a Titan II had exploded in its silo because of a wrench that had fallen from the grasp of a mechanic and punctured the first stage fuel tank.

The fuel was hypergolic Aerozine 50 (hydrazine and unsymmetrical dimethyl-hydrazine), a substance that upon contact with the oxidising agent (Nitrogen Tetroxide) creates instant ignition.

Miraculously, the silo was evacuated with no fatalities that was until an explosion occurred at 03:00 hrs the following day, blowing the 740-ton silo closure door several hundred yards away together with the second stage fuel tank and the nuclear warhead.

The second stage exploded as it egressed the silo propelling the warhead onto nearby farmland. Fortunately, the warhead remained intact; unfortunately, a specialist airman, one of two sent to investigate the condition and chemical stability of the silo was killed by the explosion. He was the only casualty.

Never underestimate the power of these mothers when they go bang! O'Hearn thought to himself.

O'Hearn signed Andrew's log to indicate that he had liaised with the Close-Down Team supervisor.

"Carry on Spike," he said, by way of a parting and then returned to the lift.

At exactly 05:30 hours, O'Hearn was seated at his Flight Director (FD) desk in the control facility, looking down upon his team of engineers seated at their terminals. An intricate ballet of technology and timing was taking place within the constraints of an ever-reducing launch window. O'Hearn's callsign was *Flight* and he was the boss.

He leant back in his chair and toggled the intercom, "Flight to Close-Down Team, Lieutenant Andrews, confirm your status."

A beep indicated that his transmission was concluded.

"Sir, we have concluded the close-down procedure. The close-down cordon is secure and I have handed responsibility for the integrity of the cordon to the ground security team. I can confirm that the cordon around the vehicle is secure and is now extended to a 1-kilometre radius around SLC-4E."

"Flight to Lieutenant Andrews received. Thank you to you and your team, the coffee is hot and it's in the pot, well done, great job, Spike!" O'Hearn said, knowing Lieutenant Andrews would now be buying breakfast for his team.

"CDT to Flight received," Andrews replied, with a chuckle.

The phone rang next to O'Hearn. He toggled the switch and was greeted by the duty meteorological supervisor, Lieutenant Kate Bergen.

"Hi, Kate, what's the news for the next 12 hours?"

"Sir, it's looking good for a scheduled launch at 08:00 hours, clear skies and low winds at the launch platform right the way up to first stage separation. The weather is likely to maintain stability for the next six to eight hours. Following that, the isobars are going to spread out as the air pressure lowers and we may encounter some squally showers heading from the Pacific as the winds pick up."

O'Hearn absorbed the data. "Thanks, Kate, it looks good for a launch. Keep me notified if any changes occur and I'd like an update one hour before the scheduled launch with a detailed forecast for the following 12 hours."

"Sir, no problem." And the line went dead.

At 07:00 hours on the button, Lieutenant Bergan updated O'Hearn. There was no change, they were good to go. O'Hearn gave the order for the launch sequence to begin and the large digital numbers on the mission control clock clicked to T minus 60 minutes and counting; the countdown had begun.

At T minus 30, O'Hearn as Flight Director called for the Flight Control Team to give a go or no go for launch. He systematically went through his checklist despite the fact he had practised this hundreds of times in simulations and had been the FD on three previous launches from the base. In return, he received a rack of goes.

At the same time, the Titan was getting itself wound up and ready to play. The misty vapours from the vent portals allowed the surplus gases to bleed off harmlessly. The almost staged, dry ice effect caught the clean rays of the new day giving the vapour a mellow pink hue that changed to gold as the shimmering sun broke higher over the horizon.

The actual launch countdown was controlled by a system known as PAGE, a mnemonic standing for *Programmable Aerospace Ground Equipment*. At T minus 15 seconds, the solid rocket motors of the launch vehicle fired and wound up to full thrust. At exactly 08:00 hours, the Titan IVB was released and growled its way from SLC-4E.

Precisely, 130 seconds into flight, the virtually empty solid motors kicked away from the body of the Titan as the first stage fired successfully. The sequence was repeated as the first stage, exhausted of its fuel fell away towards the glistening ocean below, allowing the second stage to ignite and carry the payload towards its final orbit.

Throughout the launch, O'Hearn received constant updates from the Flight Dynamics Officer (known as FIDO) responsible for the overall trajectory of the launch and the Guidance Procedures Officer (known as Guidance) whose job was to oversee the onboard navigation and guidance software.

The bird was hot to trot. O'Hearn relaxed slightly as the GOES 7/KH-12 satellite successfully deployed from the husk of the payload fairing. Highly encrypted data immediately began to flow back to Earth as the planet's newest and most highly secret satellite hung motionless in a geostationary orbit 322 kilometres above 49° 3'N 2° 20'W.

Chapter 12
Highway 101

Gus Ward belched as he gazed towards the direction of the Pacific Ocean nearly five kilometres away. Eating junk food was playing havoc with his digestive system and the cheap coffee was fizzing his stomach lining away.

His Dodge 4x4 pickup was parked on the shoulder of Highway 101 with Gus' ample frame perched on the bonnet, facing in the magnetic direction of the AFB with the town of Lompoc to the left and Vandenberg Village to the right.

Gus had been here since yesterday, waiting for the launch, just in case, some wise-ass on the base tried to pull a fast one and bring the launch forward by a day. Right on the advertised button the launch had taken place, even so, Gus was somewhat startled to see the plume rise from the launch pad.

Gus quickly threw his mug of steaming coffee away to his right and spat his cheese bagel to the four winds. After freezing his ass off for the second day his patience was paying dues.

Gus' digital camcorder was pre-aligned on the magnetic bearing of the pads. It was a Japanese design that was state-of-the-art and capable of producing an image comprising nearly 40 million pixels, enabling any captured image to be digitally enhanced for examination.

He clicked the remote activation switch, and the camera began to digitally record the initial phase of the launch that would reap the greatest detail before the bird went too far out of visual range.

The tripod was a specially designed motor-driven pan and tilt system smooth as glass that was linked through an intelligent management program to follow any image captured by any type of mounted optical device on the tripod plate. The monster lens impassively tracked and recorded the beast in all its glory.

Gus guesstimated that the rocket had been launched from one of the Titan SLCs, depending on which one would give him a fair idea of the maximum lift-off poundage and could lead to the payload being narrowed down.

Even from this distance, he could feel the vibrations created by the violence of the controlled release of power from the rocket motors as they brutally thrust the millions of dollars of expendable hardware away from the surface of the planet.

The relentless and ferocious power roared unforgivingly through his chest as though it were a hollow drum to be pounded. The noise engulfed everything and drowned out the everyday background cacophony in a display of godlike disdainful superiority for its surroundings. It was genuinely awesome!

Birds scattered in disorientated shock as the noise swelled, driven almost to complete panic by the sustained crescendo.

Gus wanted the best imagery he could get of the design of the payload fairing. He would study it later to look for anything in the design that would make it obvious that the advertised payload was different from other such pieces of hardware.

That would mean only one thing; that the government had lied to the American people! What a scoop, he could even get some national coverage and open a real can of worms.

"Whoa!" Gus said to himself.

Hold those dreams of fame, fortune and notoriety for just a minute longer.

The rocket turned from its vertical trajectory and began a slow rolling manoeuvre onto its back as the guidance systems instructed the flight and attitude control systems to alter their pitch and angle.

Gus kept filming up until the boosters separated from the main body and the first stage continued to push the rock out of the atmosphere. Only the bright glow of the engines was now visible as the angle of the rocket denied him any other view.

Gus had wished that he could have gotten physically closer to the damn base but the security was always high and became intolerable to someone like Gus. He was waiting for the opportunity to capture as much detail of a delivery system, in the hope of exposing something other than the vanilla PR that the government fed the public.

Gus had come to take a close interest in this particular launch following a casual comment made by a close buddy of his, Ruben Jacobs, who worked as a civilian contractor at Vandenberg AFB. Ruben had told him a couple of months before that this launch was scheduled as a military communications deployment.

Nothing unusual with that; even Gus who made his living through investigative journalism couldn't see anything hidden under the bed sheets with that one.

It was only when Ruben, laced with more than a few Coors beers, let slip that the launch was being overseen solely by USAF personnel and there was a really heavy security blanket being placed over the launch.

Despite being a military comms satellite (and therefore, a spy satellite), this had struck Ruben as unusual. It struck Gus as a potential lead and one that he could do some work on.

He, soon afterwards, went on the net and to one of his usual sites that listed scheduled launches from the Kennedy Space Centre and from Vandenberg AFB. Gus found that the launch was advertised and shown on the list as the deployment of a military communications platform.

The next time he met Ruben, his buddy had told him that the faring on the rocket had been modified due to the configuration of the payload. Ruben knew nothing more and had only come by this information because he had overheard a couple of the flyboys talking in a corridor in the engineering facility.

Ruben's office backed onto the corridor and the ceiling-level sash window was always open. The USAF engineers didn't realise anyone could overhear them. The corridor was empty, and they didn't think to scan around; it was just a conversation between work colleagues walking to their office discussing a development in the programme.

When Ruben later spoke to Gus at their weekly beer meet in town and mentioned the conversation to him, it had got Gus' antennae twitching.

Ruben had in the past always passed on gems of useful intelligence that enabled Gus to dig around and piece together enough conjecture to make a story seem credible.

Gus was a self-proclaimed investigative journalist. He had no recognised journalistic training and had never been employed by a newspaper or TV station in his life. But hey, one day he decided to re-invent himself and combined his interest in government cover-ups with his knowledge of the Internet to set up his own website and hey presto!

The money came rolling in. The site was popular with over 2,000 hits a day, and the advertisers were happy to have their name attached to such a well-visited corner of the web and paid Gus accordingly. Life was sweet.

Unbeknownst to Gus, his interest in Vandenberg AFB had not gone unnoticed. Gus was no soldier. Weighing in at 220 pounds, he was a cholesterol magnet living on full-cream sugared coffee and high-fat junk food; the trade-off for long hours spent on the road.

In short, he soon came to the attention of base security, who noted his presence as a matter of routine and ran the usual checks.

The AFB security was such that they had legitimate access to several public record indices including the state and national driving permit and vehicle licensing databases. Gus' licence tags were run through the system, which showed that he lived locally to the south in Santa Barbara in a rented condo.

Gus was positively identified from his licence photo and a background check was commissioned. The check established that Gus ran an internet site from home which was dedicated to the promotion of conspiracy theories on purported secret government projects.

The site had a solid reputation and was not considered to be in the cranky corner with all the other conspiracy sites, because unlike some of his associates, Gus was not an idiot.

The work he had submitted, showed an impressive amount of research and actually drew conclusions based on some factual detail as opposed to the usual guesswork found in the written pieces of his peers.

Due to a recent memorandum from the base commander (a two-star tipped to soon be getting his third Generals star) the base security report was routinely forwarded to the CIA at Langley together with a number of other security intelligence reports.

Langley ran their own checks and found nothing to Gus' detriment; he even paid his taxes. The report was noted, endorsed and filed; the assessment of Gus himself and his appearance at a routine launch was not thought to be of any consequence in terms of a security threat to the base.

Unbeknownst to Langley, they were not the only ones reading their own mail.

The decision had been made. Gus Ward was a danger to the security integrity of the operation. Mallory had been outvoted on this decision more so based on the clock winding down and the risks of potential compromise rather than hard facts.

And not for the first time, Mallory had to walk away. The only moral respite he could salvage was that he was against

Gus' life being taken; he didn't even know the guy, but life is life.

Gus returned home feeling very happy with his trip to the pads. Gus had felt an almost familiar feeling that he only experienced when tired or hung over; his heart rate would increase rapidly, and his left arm and his jaw would ache.

It would normally take around an hour and a half for the symptoms to ease with his heart rate increasing to around 180 beats per minute: his PB was 201.

Gus decided to sit his fat ass into his favourite chair and ride this mother out and popped a couple of prescription Flecainide Acetate tablets to bring his heart rate down.

He went to the fridge, popped a couple of cubes into his whisky and flicked on the TV.

For Gus, though the United States of America had taken the bold and uncompromising (and difficult) decision to carry out an end-of-life mission against a fellow American.

The ice melted. A gram of near-pure cocaine bled gently into Gus' whisky, followed by another dram. Then, the chemistry kicked in.

Gus had Supraventricular Tachycardia (SVT) which was a thing around fit teens and children. Gus clearly wasn't one of those dudes and his heart was now doing a cartoon thump below his t-shirt.

So rapid was his heart pumping that it ceased to be efficient and could not give the body a free flow of oxygenated blood around the body and more importantly, carry oxygen to his organs.

Gus' heart must have reached the point of maximum endurance and despite a desperate subconscious will to live on, it just simply couldn't cope anymore; the ice cubes were adding a fatal dynamic.

And so, Gus felt the rush of the coke, a drug he'd never consciously taken. He gently started to slip into a euphoric dream as his fast-beating chest finally gave out. What had once been the beating heart of an infant, slowly beat one last and final time.

Chapter 13
The Karma Kickback

Mallory had been in his office since 07:00 that morning, having spent a considerable amount of the weekend in touch with a high-ranking contact in MPSB, the Metropolitan Police Special Branch.

They had discussed the near tragic assault on Jayne, and Tom's timely intervention. It was agreed that the victim and her knight in shining armour should remain out of any official investigation; their parts to be considered non-existent.

Mallory had negotiated this outcome, so as not to unnecessarily ruffle any of his MPSB friend's feathers and had not needed to show his sublime authority and serve a supporting edict signed by the PM.

Mallory was a detail man and had already briefed the PM on the security implications that could arise at this late stage. The PM had enjoyed Mallory's visit to Chequers on Friday night and had insisted that he had stayed overnight, a prudent move since the Bushmills were flowing as freely as it was.

The PM was totally supportive of Mallory's strategy and directly issued a written authority to guarantee the utmost compliance from the police to maintain the cover story. He justified it as a matter of the highest importance in the interests of national security.

Mallory surmised that the best route was to rely on the arrogance of the street thugs involved, who for reasons of ego would never admit that they were so incompetent as to have been so severely injured by just one man.

Street credibility would insist that their emerging version of events would reflect those rival villains had set upon them. The code of the street was strong and demanded that they did not disclose to the police the identities of their numerous assailants.

Saturday morning was spent at the office, speaking to Commander MacMillan of the MPSB. The commander's rank entitled him to a secure Brent 2 phone at home through which Mallory had discussed the matter with him.

The commander, in turn, spoke to the Detective Chief Superintendent of the area who covered the scene of the attack on Jayne. He outlined the MPSB's interest in the incident as the individuals involved were believed to be strongly connected with the right-wing fascist British National Party.

The commander stressed that in the opinion of the MPSB the BNP was in the process of obtaining weapons and explosives. The intention was to start a nationwide campaign of intimidation, shootings and bombings against prominent members of the ethnic communities.

Part of what MacMillan told the DCS was true. The intelligence MacMillan was privy to indicated that the BNP had not yet acquired sufficient weapons. They were literally keeping their powder dry until the arsenal was sufficiently stocked. That was another story based on information coming in from the CIS, the Commonwealth of Independent States and the former Soviet Bloc.

The DCS, in turn, prioritised the gathering of evidence including DNA and forensic examinations on the weapons found on the two men.

By Monday mid-morning, the DCS was rewarded with the preliminary results of the DNA taken from Lee and Den after they were admitted directly to the hospital from the scene of the attack. Whilst in the hospital, it became clear that the two men were not simple victims and sufficient grounds existed for their arrest and detention.

A hospital custody procedure was completed. Lee and Den became men under arrest, albeit ones who couldn't go anywhere even if they desperately wanted to escape, their injuries were incapacitating.

In keeping with the hospital custody process, post-arrest DNA samples were obtained from the men's saliva and taken to Paddington Green Police Station for storage before examination; maintaining the continuity of evidence of the exhibits as the samples had now become.

The hastened analysis of the DNA exhibits brought about by Mallory's contact with the MPSB indicated that Lee and Den were now strong suspects in the rape of a German exchange student in March.

A comprehensive DNA profile would now be undertaken to match more rigorous sampling aside from the saliva samples taken from the two detainees, who, after initial treatment, had been moved to the hospital wing of HMP Wandsworth.

By lunchtime, the Metropolitan Police forensic science laboratory had also matched the barrelling of the handgun to several bullets recovered from the body of a 48-year-old Nigerian male in Stepney. At the time when the male was gunned down, it was believed that he had been simply hit in the crossfire of shots exchanged between rival factions over the control of drug turf.

Ironically, Den and Lee had not been involved in the shooting and had only got hold of the gun as part payment on the car belonging to the banker they'd robbed and stabbed.

The *caught in crossfire* theory was now believed to be wrong, especially, in the light of the information from the MPSB. The Nigerian had recently sued his former employers for racial discrimination having been passed over for promotion.

He had won his case and received a substantial settlement, not to mention extensive coverage in the London Evening Standard.

The Nigerian's bitter employer had used underworld contacts to carry out the *hit* and Den and Lee would carry the can.

Even if they grassed to the cops, the overwhelming evidence against the boys would be difficult to explain *("Oh yeah, it was part payment for a geezer we stabbed and killed")*, overturning the conviction and convicting the real hit man was nothing more than a pipe dream. The boys were going down.

Sometimes, Karma has a funny way of balancing the books.

Den and Lee were getting deeper into the shit and the Metropolitan Police forensic science laboratory had yet to examine the knife.

A search warrant was executed on Sunday morning at Lee's home address. He lived in a bed-sit in a run-down and depressed street just off the King's Road. As the warrant had primarily been issued to search for firearms, a Metropolitan Police Tactical Firearms Unit had effected the entry into the bed-sit at 05:30 hours.

The door to Lee's digs had shattered as the kinetic door ram had torn it away from the frame and architrave. The flat was unoccupied, and the smell of dank stuffiness was all-pervading; the windows were closed and the ancient radiator was moist with condensation.

A used plate with half-eaten food was on the worktop and the sink was full of old mugs, cutlery and dishes, together with a few discarded cigarette ends bobbing around in the grey dishwater.

The team leader of the TFU winked to the MPSB Detective Sergeant who was now in charge of the scene. He was relieved that his godlike work here was done. He was eager to take his flock of men in black away from this grubby little shithole.

The MPSB DS was also none too impressed with the possibility of spending the rest of his day sifting through the stinking mess of a festering druggie gaff. There was nothing else to be done, the professionals needed to be brought in for this one.

He picked up his mobile and arranged for a search team to be brought in. By 06:20 hours, a team was meticulously and systematically taking the flat apart in a thorough anti-terrorist search.

At 09:15 hours, two officers took off the doors to the kitchen unit under the sink, removing an array of circa 1970s

Flash and other fading gems from that era in their bloated cardboard packaging; the contents were swollen by the ingress of moisture into the powder.

The surrounding clutter was removed and the officers saw signs of what they believed to be a *hide*. Floorboards had been sawn to create a concealment between the floor joists and were resting in situ, having simply been pushed back into place.

The search team commander was called to assess the next step, and in due course, the two officers checked the crudely disguised cache for anti-handling devices; none were found.

The area under the sink had been photographed at each stage of the search process by a SOCO (scenes of crime officer), who was an expert in the taking of evidential photographs and exhibits.

The concealment though amateurish was still one that would have been effective to any search but the most thorough. Everyone knew that you didn't keep legitimate items in a hide. The team's anticipation was growing.

The two lengths of floorboard were lifted one at a time, held in place by nothing more complex than the tongue and groove routing of the floorboards themselves. Once removed, the search team officer shone her torch into the exposed hide between the floor joists. She saw the damning evidence that would put the former occupant of this squalid dump away for a couple of decades.

A scrunched-up copy of the Standard (dated only a few days ago) that had partially opened up and outwards like some bizarre flowering paper bloom. Inside the paper were five clear plastic bank bags, each containing 10 rounds of .45 ammunition together with a single magazine clip.

Later examination by the forensic science lab would show that these rounds were the same production batch as those found in Lee's handgun. The examination of the handgun was also to reveal that Den had, at some point, handled the weapon. The boys had some explaining to do.

Worse was to come for Den, when the knife found at the scene was matched to one that had been used to recently fatally stab a merchant banker. The blade had not been properly cleaned or sanitised after the robbery. It just been given a superficial Hollywood wipe that works well in the movies but doesn't stand up to the might of modern-day forensic examination.

The banker's DNA was extracted from the crusted blood within the blade housing of the knife. Another murder was on its way to being solved.

Chapter 14
Update

Mallory walked into the general office from his adjoining executive suite just after 8:00 hours, and found Tom and Jayne sitting at their desks chatting over a cup of coffee. Jayne smiled as Mallory sat and joined them wincing slightly from the punch to her cheek she had received from Lee.

"Hi, Boss," Jayne said, a little embarrassed by the bruising on her face.

"Jayne," said Mallory, letting the words drift into silence. A smile creased his face. "Is your toe bruised as well, from what Tom tells me you'd be pretty good on the rugby field taking a conversion."

Jayne looked down and grinned. The smile faded as her head came back up and was replaced by a steely defiance in her eyes.

"I honestly thought that I was going to be raped and beaten. They were a pair of filthy…pigs. When Tom—" the words faded as her voice trembled slightly with the emotion brimming up to the surface.

With her head bowed, Jayne said, "When Tom appeared, I knew that I was going to be okay. I was so frightened, and I felt so helpless."

Mallory leaned forward and said gently, "You didn't know that help was on its way and you still fought; that takes courage. You knew that if you were going down it would be fighting and with honour. Most people in that situation would have let the fear take them over, you controlled it and turned it around against them. That is the true measure of who you really are."

Jayne could feel her eyes moistening as Mallory spoke, genuinely grateful for this man's compassion and kindness.

"Thanks, Boss," she whispered.

Tom watched as Mallory's compliment of Jayne's courage filled in the gaps her self-esteem had eroded over the weekend during the continuous playing and replaying of the whole nightmare. Jayne brought her head back up and squared her petite shoulders as if casting off an unwanted burden.

"Time to freshen up, then I'll make the coffee!" Jayne declared and walked to the toilet.

Tom and Mallory's eyes met.

"Nice one Boss," said Tom. "She is a fighter, that one, but as strong as she thinks she is, the self-doubt was starting to take its toll. What you told her then, really hit home and what's best is, that it's true. Jayne is a gutsy little thing."

A few minutes later, Jayne came back into the office, looking thoroughly more together and invigorated.

Jayne replenished the coffees, taking a little extra care this morning with Mallory's hazelnut ground variety. Mallory savoured the aroma holding the mug in both hands between the forefinger and thumb and sipping carefully at the steaming brew.

Mallory paused and then turned towards the two expectant faces of his subordinates. "I think I should bring you up to speed on the developments in relation to the two men arrested in the early hours of Saturday morning." He then began to relate the events from his discussion with the PM up until the latest discoveries by the MPSB.

During the briefing, Jayne had turned away slightly from Mallory's direction and was facing towards the window with her head resting gently against her wrist and palm. Jayne's mind absorbed the list of disgusting atrocities committed by the two. It was repugnant, especially, as the police were now linking them to that sickening assault on the elderly couple. What a tragedy!

Tom sat impassively throughout, reliving inside the sense of dread he had felt at the sight of Jayne's tiny frame being manhandled by those brutes. He inwardly smiled as Mallory revealed that the prognosis from the surgeons was not good.

Both men were permanently disabled, Lee's kneecap was beyond repair and consideration was being given to amputating above the knee as a post-operation infection was risking the entire limb. Lee would also have a permanent speech impediment arising from the damage to the nerves in the jaw and tongue.

Den was similarly in bad shape and had lost the use of his right arm due to massive neurological damage caused by the injury. Tom smiled when Mallory also mentioned that Den was no longer able to sire any pups.

"I'm travelling to Washington at 1 pm, and I will return on Thursday. I want to have an in-house briefing on Friday, that's the 23rd."

Mallory turned to Tom. "I want you to bring Austin in on this. He is from your old mob and what gives him the edge is, that he was actually born and raised in Jersey."

"Good call, Boss. I worked with Austin on a number of jobs in Iraq and Afghanistan, he is a solid operator and one sharp cookie." Tom paused. "Last I heard, he was in Syria tracking down ISIS leadership."

"Yes, I know. That's why I want him. He and his team have been extremely ruthless in extracting intelligence from the grassroots and have had some serious success. I know he won't be too impressed being taken off his current deployment, but that's just too bad. Get Austin here, fresh and good to go. No ifs or buts!" Malory, the boss, had spoken and Austin would soon be on board.

Chapter 15
Syria

As the conversation between Malory and Tom was taking place, Austin and the three other SBS operators were just about to go into contact. The team were about to extract intelligence from a goat kisser, whom they had observed, departing the address of a known ISIS commander in Al Qaryatayn.

The goat kisser, called Husnain, was unaware that he was being targeted by Austin's team as he jumped onto his moped and sped away into the night in a cloud of dust, riding off the same way in which he had ridden. This was to be one of his last tactical mistakes.

He was too preoccupied with the thought of shagging his 14-year-old child bride, and he could feel himself starting to rise in anticipation. The fact that the young girl was an unwilling partner was of no consequence to Husnain; a quick beating if she showed any reluctance always forced her into submission.

Husnain had just been ordered to take a USB stick to Homs, just over 100 kilometres away and was tasked to avoid the main Damascus to Homs highway as this was considered too vulnerable to predator drone strikes. This meant Husnain would travel mainly off-road, and then join the road at Sadad and into Homs. He reckoned two days in total which was agreed by the commander in Al Qaryatayn.

Husnain was a mile away, his moped beyond the hearing of anyone in Al Qaryatayn. As he rounded, a rocky outcrop and down into a Wadi, the silent round shattered a rib and punctured his right lung causing his body to spin as he tumbled off the moped.

He breathed in sharply, pain and confusion flowing through him. He heard the moped's engine being switched off as footsteps slowly crunched towards him. In a panic, he fumbled in the darkness for his AK but it was beyond his reach still strapped to the moped.

The Wadi had been specifically selected and was the perfect location to carry out a takedown. No one apart from Husnain had used it in the past three days, and there was no ground sign to indicate that it had been used in years.

Austin and his team had followed Husnain back to his blockwork and clay digs in Al Baridah and had endured listening to the pig slap his child bride into submission before raping her.

It was one of the toughest things Austin and his team had ever done by doing nothing; the only consolation was that this pig would soon be dead.

One day earlier, SIGINT (signals intelligence) from the ECHELON surveillance programme at RAF Menwith Hill in North Yorkshire had detected and decoded a 128-bit encrypted mobile message between Al Qaryatayn and Homs.

The message indicated that a package would be couriered between both locations and contained significant intelligence relating to the supply of weapons and funding to ISIS. The decision was made by the intelligence agencies on both sides of the Atlantic to intercept and secure the package.

The sharp end of that decision was now crouched over Husnain in the form of Austin and Ash, whilst Nick and Jim took up positions covering the approaches from the north and south. All of the guys had adequate in-country language skills, but Ash was the fluent Arab speaker on the team.

The dawning realisation that this was not going to be a good night out slowly spread through Hasnain's body and he began to shake and whimper; *a bit like his child bride did*, thought Ash.

"Shut the fuck up!" Ash whispered menacingly to Husnain in Arabic, delivering a deliberate punch to his broken rib.

Husnain momentarily passed out and was brought back around by a sharp slap across the face.

"Where is the USB?" Ash asked. "I…I don't know what you mean," Husnain lied almost choking with fear.

Ash coolly looked at Husnain and very slowly and deliberately said, "I will fucking cut you open to find it. Your call. I'm guessing, I'll start by looking in your fucking ball bag—" Ash drew his knife and let Husnain feast his eyes on the blade as Ash slowly took the knife south.

"No, no, please. I have it, just please do not hurt me," said Husnain close to tears, his chest painfully heaving as he fought to contain his fear.

His shaking hands fumbled as he removed a leather cord from around his neck and showed Ash and Austin the USB dangling at the cord's end. "Please, take it, and let me go. I have a wife who loves me very much, don't kill me, please."

"Yeah," said Ash. "We know, we heard you rape the kid last night. No more, never again." With that Ash put his hand over Hasnain's mouth and sank the blade into his chest directly into the heart.

It felt almost too humane to kill the goat kisser this quickly.

"Okay guys," said Austin over the net. "Nick and Jim, strap the moped to one of your quad bikes. Ash and I will white-phoss the body. Meet at the FRV (Forward Rendezvous) at 01:00. All call signs, acknowledge."

Chapter 16
RAF Farnborough

The door of the parked Range Rover slammed shut in the private aircraft car park at RAF Farnborough. The Rangy rocked as Austin sat heavily in the passenger seat throwing his kit onto the back seat. His team in utmost secrecy had been rapidly extracted from Syria to RAF Akrotiri in Cyprus.

Austin then did the three Ss (shit, shower and shave) and then was taken to an awaiting Cessna Citation Latitude which was registered to a brass plate trust company in Bahrain.

Should anyone choose to do a bit of digging it was, in fact, owned by another bona fide trust company from the Bahamas and used as a front for a small number of aircraft His Majesty's government wanted to keep off the books.

The trade-off was HMG were happy to turn a blind eye to certain peccadilloes the beneficial billionaire owner of the company may have. But cross the line and you might fall off your yacht in the Mediterranean, or commit suicide in your around-the-clock guarded cell.

In any case, Austin was back home in an indecent haste. Even Husnain's ashes were still warm.

"What the fuck are you thinking?" Austin growled through clenched teeth at Tom. "I was halfway through a fucking mission in fucking Syria and I get told to fucking return. Not even a chance to hand over to whoever the fuck is taking my place. That's a bad fucking operational process."

"Good to see you too mate!" said Tom, inwardly chuckling to himself as to how he was going to extract much beerage out of Austin for being so wronged for calling him in. "How did the boys take it?"

"I last saw them throwing beer down their necks in the sergeant's mess at RAF Akrotiri. Happy as pigs in shit." A faint smile crept across Austin's face. "In fairness, they deserved it after three months in Syria."

"Tom, I know you from old and I know you don't fuck around, so, what's so fucking important? What's happening?"

For once, Tom was solemn and quip-free. It was something, Austin found more than a little disconcerting.

"I promise you, Austin, something incredible is about to go down. I'm taking you to a place where everything will be explained to you."

Austin looked out of the window, his mind working furiously to explain what Tom had just said. As the Range Rover growled along the A325 towards the M3 and as if on cue, the dark clouds that had been looming, suddenly opened, and rain smashed against the windscreen.

Chapter 17
Briefing Austin

Tom swung the Range Rover through the gates of Corporate Trading International and parked next to Jayne's Porsche.

"Leave your kit in the car, Austin, you can skip at my place, mate."

"Cheers, Tom," Austin replied. "A lot of parking for a small number of cars, mate."

Tom led the way to the lift, once inside he said, "I'm going to introduce you to David Mallory. He is a super smart spook and he is in charge of this operation, which is a combined effort between us and the Americans."

"How serious is this job?" Austin liked to ask blunt obvious questions but was unprepared for Tom's reply.

"Well, pretty serious. We launched a modified KH 12 satellite a few days ago from Vandenberg, its sole purpose is this mission," Tom casually replied.

"You fucking what?" said Austin, just as the lift smoothly slowed and the doors opened.

There stood Mallory. "So pleased to meet you, Austin. Tom speaks very highly of you," said Mallory, extending his hand to Austin.

"Pleasure is mine, Boss. And don't believe anything Tom tells you, he lies like a hairy egg." Smiled Austin, wondering what the fuck was going on.

Mallory grinned and shook his head. "This way, Austin. Tom, you too."

Almost exactly one hour later, Tom and Austin walked out of Mallory's office.

As Tom left, he turned to Mallory and said, "We're going to have a wet debrief. (The parlance for a post-op debrief with beerage or better). Fancy joining us?"

Mallory smiled, turned slightly, opened the bottom drawer of his desk, pulled out a bottle of Bushmills and placed it on his desk.

"Only in spirit," Mallory quipped. "Enjoy, you've both earned it. I'm off home. Catch you both tomorrow."

As Mallory left, Tom walked across to a large lounge area looking over the Thames and handed Austin a chilled beer from the fridge.

"A quick one of these before we take on the bosses Bushmills!" Austin sunk into the sumptuous sofa popped the ring on his can and took a long swig. "Ah fuck, that's better!"

"We're safe to speak out here, even though that's a big sheet of glass," he said pointing to the window with his beer.

"The window has frequency agile vibration to resonate the glass. The frequency shifts and doesn't repeat, so it can't be tuned out by anyone trying to eavesdrop."

"Some fucking gig you've got going on here, Tom."

Chapter 18
Final Stages

Tom delivered the briefing from the conference room at Corporate Trading International which was simultaneously transmitted to Colonel Mike O'Hearn and Lieutenant Spike Andrews at Vandenberg AFB.

They would solely be real-time monitoring the KH-12. Also to Air Vice Marshal Jonny Adams at RAF Menwith Hill whose team would be crunching the incoming data from the KH-12.

The plan was for this data to be stripped apart and analysed by Adams' football pitch-sized platform of supercomputers to determine the nature of the event that led to and indeed will lead to Carter slipping back in time.

The stakes were now much higher as the SBS team would be following Carter into the anomaly with no guarantee of ever being able to return. A sobering thought for all of those concerned and the impetus for solving the single most important discovery arguably in human history; the ability to move through time.

Jayne sat in the room with Malory and Tom's troopers. A second SBS team, all men that Tom's crew had worked with before, had been brought on board. They will be led by Ash who had been with Austin on the Al Qaryatayn operation in Afghanistan a couple of weeks before. The role of Ash's crew was to RV with Tom and his team at the egress back to their own time.

For ease of reference, Tom's team was referred to as Sierra 22 and Ash's team Zulu 55 as both the phonetics of the letters and numbers were distinct and would make each callsign aurally distinct too.

A few hurdles lay ahead.

"Fucking big ones!" as Austin had quite succinctly mentioned to Tom.

Namely, a means of recreating the as-yet-unknown event had to be discovered and engineered. Then, Ash and his team would need to be inserted and remain on target until Tom and the surviving members could converge on what would become Carter's cottage.

They would, then, need to fight their way back to the site of the original anomaly to have any hope of returning.

"Quite straightforward really," Tom quipped to lighten the mood of the briefing.

The mood soon darkened when Tom moved on to the operational contingencies and in particular OPSEC or Operational Security. It was clear that no identifiable trace of the teams could be left in the past, this included equipment and personnel.

The mere fact that the DNA would be left was a major concern but was discounted as any profiling could not be attempted for several decades in the future of the infiltration. Thus, by that time, any traces would be of no use, such was the extent of the security surrounding what the SBS simply called *The Job*.

Tom reiterated *surviving members*. The operation demanded that *no identifiable trace* could be left of either equipment or the personnel. The brutal truth was there would be no John Wayne heroics carrying fallen buddies home; the bodies would be disposed of and any seriously injured operatives could not be left to fall into enemy hands.

They all knew what this meant. The method of disposal would be done using white phosphorus flares which burn at 5000 degrees Fahrenheit; hotter than the surface of the sun. Thus, reducing a body to ash or metal to its melted state. Tom nodded to Austin's team who had done much to the AQ courier during their last Op in Syria.

After two and a half hours, the briefing was concluded, and the teams clicked into mission prep mentality and purposely went away to carry out their final preparations. The mantra of *check and test, check and test* was the drumbeat of the professional SF soldier.

Both the Sierra and Zulu teams had spent several days on weapons familiarity with a number of German WWII guns and could now strip; clean and fire an array of kit.

To a man, they chose the Sig Saur M17 which delivered 19 mm Parabellum round at a blistering 1,190 feet per second out of a 21-round mag. Each man also opted for the Heckler & Koch HK417 assault rival with the folding butt. This variant could fire a 7.62 round, affectionately known as the de-limber; no further explanation is required.

Chapter 19
The Build-Up

The ground team comprised Tom, Austin, Nick and Jim. The time for briefings and planning phases was now over. The moment of decades of preparation and planning was coming to a head.

Billions of pounds and dollars of covert investment had been expended. With a resignation to the inevitable and unknown that nothing more could be done. Literally, the future was in the hands of a four-man SBS team and never in history had such a burden been placed on any soldier.

If they failed, the invasion of Europe would in all likelihood be compromised costing thousands of lives and history as written would be unequivocally changed.

As the clock ticked towards Carter's time slip, the only known piece of reliable information, the team were ready and prepared. They were dressed in genuine German uniforms which had been saved and preserved following the end of WWII when the mission emerged, and the first custodian was appointed.

Mary Forrester realised someone would need to follow Carter into whatever lay ahead, and set about securing all clothing and equipment to ensure that the outward authenticity of the operatives would be unquestioned.

Tom and his team were also equipped with cutting-edge blunt weaponry such as explosives and guns in support of the standard issue equipment of the Waffen SS.

The Waffen SS had been chosen as the cover the team would adopt as they were feared amongst all levels and ranks of the German army and even the Gestapo. You would have to be a brave soul to question one of these bastards, so the thinking went.

It was determined that this psychological barrier would be a tactical advantage in discouraging approaches from either the occupying military forces or the civilian population. Plus, Tom and his team had enough gold sovereigns and period German Marks to buy their way out of most other situations.

The simple fact was that regardless of all the planning and technical support, once they followed Carter and crossed over in time, getting back was in the hands of others if it was at all possible.

The psychometric testing of the team showed them all to be very resilient to stress and highly mission focussed. A powerful combination when mixed in with their Special Forces training and extreme levels of fitness; the closest a human can get to being a deadly machine.

The simple extraction plan was for the team, Carter or simply any surviving members to make their way back to the point of ingress in Jersey and wait for operatives to RV. The chosen location was Carter's cottage which in 1944 was unoccupied and in a state of neglect.

"Ground asset confirms, the subject has left the home address. All call signs, acknowledge."

In response, each operative pressed the click button on their PTTs three times to acknowledge the transmission. It was their covert and silent way to do so and reduce any avoidable talking.

Two clicks meant *No* three clicks meant *Yes*. The same number of clicks to letters in the word; count the clicks and that is the answer to your question.

The movement was confirmed by the KH-12 in geostationary orbit which transmitted the exceptionally clear image of Carter leaving his cottage with his dog for a late-night walk. The imagery was being viewed in real time, both at Langley in West Virginia and at Mallory's HQ at St Kathryn's Docks.

The array of Cray computers at RAF Menwith Hill (which in reality was an American NSA facility) was focussed on this task alone, processing billions of pieces of data. Anticipation began to mount on both sides of the Atlantic.

The SBS team monitored Carter as he passed close by following Fizz, his dog, who bounded ahead into the darkness. There was only one simple option that they now had and that was to stay close to Carter, unnoticed and silent.

To do this, the team were using a skill called *stalking*. It is mostly used by snipers and close observation platoon operatives to quietly and covertly approach their hide or in rare circumstances follow a target through a wood or forest.

The skill was mentally demanding as it required total concentration. Also, it was physically challenging as every step required complete muscular control to feel for solid footing to prevent too much weight being applied at once which could cause a twig to snap or crack and make a noise.

Any unnatural noise or noise out of place could be a deadly mistake for the soldier stalking.

The team had no choice. The plan was simple. They had to keep close to Carter as no one knew when and where exactly he would slip through, just that he would do so very soon. Most importantly, how long would the door behind Carter remain open?

Miles overhead, the KH-12 began to detect an inconsistent reading. Inconsistent compared with the mountains of accumulated data for the area. Just little flutters on the baseline gravity for the target zone.

The data was immediately crunched by the Cray computers and algorithms filtered out any noise from the readings. Then the readings stopped.

"Fuck! What was that?" Rob Charles said, leaning forward on his desk back at RAF Menwith Hill as if the act of moving closer to the screen would cough up an answer.

"I saw that too," said Air Vice Marshal Johnny Adams. "Rob, confirm that Langley is on this."

A few seconds later, Rob replied, "They are, Sir."

"Then, eyes down and look in." the AVM said quietly.

Simultaneously, at Vandenberg AFB Spike Andrews turned to Mike O'Hearn and said, "Boss, some fucking weird shit is happening."

No sooner was this said, than a gravity spike appeared.

"Holy shit, Boss! Look at this!" Charles said as he turned to the AVM, his voice creeping up an octave as he spoke.

On the screen a precise location was identified, some 50 meters ahead of where Carter was walking. The change in readings began to flood in.

On the ground, Tom and his team received the information. Despite their extensive exposure to stress and conflict to a man, their heart rates began to increase as their bodies reverted to nature's response to danger: the fight or flight instinct. With grim resolve, they pressed on without a pause.

Ahead, Tom saw through his NVGs what looked like a mini aurora borealis approximately 50 meters ahead of Carter. He quietly lifted his Gen4s and the lights were gone, explaining why Carter continued towards the anomaly; he couldn't see it.

Tom keyed his throat mike and passed on the information to the rest of the SBS team who had noted the light show through their own NVGs. Clicks were received in response.

Back at RAF Menwith Hill, Rob Charles and the AVM watched the mounting flood of data.

The AVM lifted the phone, "Sir. Oh okay, John. Something is definitely happening. The readings from the KH-12 are building and the subject is on foot towards the anomaly. The SBS team are also on foot close by to the subject. Will do, speak soon, John." With that, he placed the phone back on its cradle and said to no one in particular, "Well that's the PM notified."

Charles turned to Adams and said, "Sir, the indications are that there is a spike in the baseline gravity at the exact point 50 metres ahead of Carter which could explain the magnetic anomaly."

"Clearly, the reason the anomaly is not visible is that the human eye can only see 0.0035% of the electromagnetic spectrum. So, the anomaly must be outside of the visible spectrum. It does make you wonder what dogs sometimes bark at when we think there's nothing there."

The AVM nodded slowly. "Whatever the physics behind what we have just seen happen, one thing is certain, slipping through time is possible. Clearly, every point in time must axiomatically coexist with every other point in time. I believe they call the theory *the block theory* whereby all dimensions exist simultaneously."

Chapter 20
The Event

On the ground, Tom and the team pressed on. There were no Star Trek laser beams or Hollywood flash and bangs, they simply walked across time following Carter.

Carter stopped. Suddenly, all the ambient noise had vanished and the lights in St Helier and across everywhere had gone off.

Fucking French! Carter thought, after all the post-Brexit shit on fishing rights, the fucking garlic-eating surrender monkeys had finally pulled the plug on our electricity supply!

But Carter's senses started to scream; this did not feel right.

At the same time, a fucking German re-enactor walked out in front of him.

"Hande hoch!" the German-clad twat said, pointing his plastic MP18 at Carter.

"Fuck off wanker, I'm looking for my dog," Carter said as he barged past.

The German hit Carter square between the shoulders with the butt of his gun.

This was totally unexpected causing Carter to hit the ground on all fours. This triggered Carter's reflex response and he thrust his heel back with enraged force using an intuitive sense of direction and struck bang on the kneecap of the fucking dressed-up wanker who spun to the ground howling in pain.

"Fuck you, twat," Carter said as the next blow took him out.

Tom watched with a smile as Carter kicked off, and then, focussed as the Wehrmacht (the armed forces of the Third Reich) took Carter away.

Tom through habit clicked his mike and relayed his observations. Unexpectedly he received clicks back and a "Roger that," from Rob Charles, RAF Menworth Hill and also acknowledged by AVM Jonny Adams.

All sides at the same time went, "Fuck!"

"Rob," the AVM said. "Check with the cousins and get their take. How the fuck can we hear the coms from a team that has gone back to 1944?"

Only the upturned physics of the moment could answer that fucking big one. The reason was going to arrive in a taxi at some point and tell all but until then stuff was clearly happening.

Carter woke up moments later in the dirt at Noirmont: hands tied behind his back. He spat dirt from his lips and tried to get up but was kicked to the ground.

"I am going to sue you fuckers!" Then, lights out.

Tom and the boys had watched as Carter was taken into a truck and driven away.

Tom's head was screaming, *Surely, if they can hear our comms they can monitor them?*

In a manner ready for rejection Tom keyed his mike, "Boss, do you have eyes on?"

"Yes," came the swift response from Mallory.

"Roger that, Boss," Tom replied, with a glee of a kid on Christmas Day!

Tom gathered his troops to brief them.

"You fucking what?" said Nick.

"Yep. We have comms." All the team perked up.

"All call signs, acknowledge." He put his finger to his lips to gesture to the team.

"Wait and see." Both sides of the Atlantic clicked.

Tom sat back heavily as the confirmations came in.

The truck rumbled on as Carter came too. His wrists were in handcuffs and his head throbbed. Slowly, he turned his head and said, "You fucking actors are so fucked," as he tried to sit up, only to be kicked in the stomach and throw up.

Through blood and mud-encrusted eyes, Carter decided in his mind to accept that this was some skewered new reality and to take in the moment with a view to planning his escape. Although shit at the time the *Resistance to Interrogation* course was now starting to kick in.

This moment of *up* was soon met by a moment of *down* as he knew what was coming next. *Sorry bollocks for the kicking you are about to receive.*

The truck pulled up hard at the entrance to Ho8. This was a collection of Hohlgangslange (tunnels built by the German occupying forces; a unique name for such tunnels built in the Channel Islands) a secret hospital tunnelled into the high point of a rock face in a central valley in St Lawrence.

It could be used also for weapon storage and a bomb-proof shelter for troops. Carter knew it, he'd been there on a school trip as a kid.

The place was as shown on the photos of the occupation, built by the German Organisation Todt some of the 6000 slaves brought into Jersey from France, Spain, Russia, Poland and Algeria to fortify the Island.

They built countless bunkers, fortifications and defensive positions at a terrible cost to the slave's lives, thousands died. At the end of the brutal construction programme, the tunnels themselves ran for over 1,000 m and could accommodate 800 patients.

In truth, Hitler was obsessed with the Channel Islands as they were British sovereign territory and ordered that they be heavily fortified.

In total, according to post-war analysis, the Channel Islands had 11 operational batteries with some 38 guns. Along an approximately 600-mile section of the strategic French Atlantic wall, there were only 37 defensive gun positions.

It has since been argued if Hitler had not fortified the Channel Islands and had instead strengthened the Normandy defences with the additional 11 operational batteries, D-Day would have failed.

The complex remained one of the best-preserved examples of Nazi engineering. Carter wondered if his experience now was an illusion, a bad stress dream. If so, it was fucking vivid.

Then, the reality hit. Carter was dragged, whilst handcuffed, to the truck's tailgate and pulled out. He managed to tuck his face away, but his right shoulder took the full impact of the fall. Nothing was broken but the fucking Germans didn't know that.

At the same time, a Kubelwagon arrived at Ho8 and a Waffen SS officer stepped out. The Wehrmacht soldiers froze as the Nazi's finest approached.

Carter watched as the officer arrogantly strolled across to the Wehrmacht soldiers. With a slight sense of smugness, he could tell from the fuckers who had brought him here, they were now clearly shitting themselves as they snapped to attention.

A very brief conversation took place which consisted mainly of a lot of stressful, "Jawhol mein Herr!" in response to acid-dipped orders.

Shortly thereafter, Carter was taken into the complex by the Wehrmacht and Waffen SS.

Tom lowered the binos and in his mind weighed up the options to attempt an assault on a well-defended and fortified position, or wait for Carter to be released or moved to another location.

It was obvious that an assault with a force as small as Tom's would not have a happy ending which would only provide more modern-day material and equipment to be compromised.

Balance that against the possibility of Carter being killed by unpleasant interrogation methods, the latter was the lesser risk.

Tom keyed his mike, "Boss, do you still have comms?"

"Yes, we do and eyes on!" said Mallory, with cool professional detachment, the kind of guy you wanted to have your back in any adverse scenario.

"I will act as your Operational Commander and will stay on post to monitor your radio comms."

"Yes, yes!" replied Tom, inwardly breathing a sigh of relief that safe hands were in play. "How so is this happening, Boss?" said Tom completely perplexed.

At the same time, he needed to know from a ground commander's perspective exactly what his communication support was together with satellite surveillance support.

"Tom, we have no idea. But I am sure that you can imagine the frantic work that is taking place at both ends of the Atlantic to answer that very question."

"Yes, yes. Can you then advise when the Kubelwagon moves or is approached? This will allow us to formulate a plan at this end and get some rest. In the absence of any other intelligence, an assault on this position will fail. Our intention will be to follow Carter upon his egress from Ho8 and carry out a RoK (Retrieve or Kill). Hopefully, recovering Carter and the material, or kill and destroy both beyond forensic recovery."

Mallory quickly absorbed Tom's transmission and agreed. A tough call, but the right decision considering the bigger picture. "Yes, yes, I agree."

"Roger that. All call signs, acknowledge."

Reassuringly, Tom heard three clicks from the guys and a, "Yes, yes," from Mallory.

Chapter 21
Ho8

SS Hauptstrurmfuhrer (Captain) Felix Von Wolff arrogantly strode into Ho8. Aryan in appearance and a fanatical Nazi born in Austria; his arrogance was almost palpable. In a perverse way, an Austrian considered themselves superior to a German, one of whom was now standing in front of him.

"Commandant (said with a click of the heels and a sharp nod, but no respect to the rank), I would like to see the possessions found on the prisoner captured at Noirmont. Bring the soldier who captured him with you to your office and some whisky, single malt none of that schnapps shit."

The short and slightly rotund commandant, Colonel Schmidt was clearly not an Aryan but being three ranks higher and addressed in this manner in front of his men, could not go unchallenged.

"May I remind you, Hauptstrurmfuhrer, I am a Colonel an Obersleutnant, and in charge of this facility. You are a Hauptstrurmfuhrer and are not! Respect the rank and not the soldier, if you must. But do not ever address me in this manner again. Do you understand?"

The blow that struck Colonel Schmidt was unexpected and brutal, delivered by Captain Von Wolff. The Wehrmacht soldiers to a man stepped forward to protect their Colonel who was considered a genuinely nice bloke amongst the troops.

Von Wolff simply stood up and snarled at the pathetic ex-butchers, bakers and candle stick makers who now only wore a uniform because of having been called up to fight for the Fuhrer; and they now dared to intimidate him!

He, of all people, a professional soldier from a family of professional soldiers. In answer, he kicked Schmidt in the stomach and knelt down, grabbing his tunic by the collar and hissed, "Malt whisky, you little Fotze. Do not ever question my authority as an officer of the SS."

Carter had observed this little interaction with tactical impartiality and a rising fear. The reality was sinking in. This wasn't a bunch of reenactors having a laugh.

The whole Ho8 complex had changed; the visitor centre was gone and the car park was gone. There was no street lighting, the driver had driven on the right and most hauntingly Carter knew this wasn't a dream, it was actually real. *Holy Christ!*

A sense of complete shock and bewilderment engulfed him, and he struggled not to throw up or shit his pants. He was in fact momentarily dehumanised.

In an extremely stressful and disorientating situation (of which this would be an unparalleled exemplar), the touchstone of resistance to interrogation training kicked in. It enabled Carter to mentally reach out and remember the training: that when all else is taken from you, your mind is still yours to control.

Von Wolff sat in the commandant's chair and in a seemingly absentminded way flicked through Colonel Schmidt's stuff on his desk.

"Dummkopf" (or fool), Von Wolff muttered, just as the Colonel walked in, sweating slightly in pain with a full glass of single malt.

"My report tomorrow will not be good for you, Colonel. You disrespected the SS and by doing so the Fuhrer. I believe you will probably be serving soon against the Russian barbarians. Go!"

In a state of shock, Colonel Schmidt walked out. He had never been a professional soldier, just a schoolmaster. Now more so than ever, he just wanted to delight his students with funny stories and try to inspire their young minds to learn and flourish amidst the beauty of the Alps. Surely, this was not happening.

The German squaddie who captured Carter had come in with the Colonel. He clearly wished he would have been looking the other way and doing up his shoelaces instead of detaining the slightly alarming man sitting before him. Carter matched his gaze and the German looked away.

Von Wolff looked at the tall, blond soldier before him subconsciously thinking of him as a fellow Ayrian.

"Explain what happened," demanded Von Wolff.

A nervously delivered recollection was given by the soldier, Herbert Schwann.

"So," said Von Wolff, "You did not believe this man, and then, without provocation, you assaulted, arrested and detained him? With no evidence?" Von Wolff shouted.

At that very moment, Herbert wanted to be absolutely anywhere else on planet Earth or the Universe than here. If the Colonel could be sent to the Russian front, merciful God what could happen to him?

"Yes, Sir, that is correct," said Herbert, clenching his jaw and looking above Von Wolff as you would on parade.

Von Wolff sat back in his chair at an angle and stroked his stubbly chin, looking intently at Schwann. He breathed out heavily and quietly said, "Stand before me Schwann."

The command was instantly complied with.

"I am impressed with your aggression, decisiveness and loyalty towards your duty, the Reich and the Fuhrer Schwann. I am promoting you to Unterfeldwebel. Staff Sergeant."

"I want you to take the prisoner to the holding cell, search him again and have all of his possessions ready for me to examine here in my office at 08:00, ready for a chat." As Von Wolff said this, he raised his glass to Carter, laughed, and then, took a deep swig of the malt. "Take him away."

That very phrase was an age-old classic interrogation technique to plant in the mind of a prisoner so as to marginalise, demoralise and dehumanise.

In human terms, you become worthless. You will even seek the friendship of your captors and consider them as true friends, apart from the fact they've locked you up, deprived you of food and water and traumatised you mentally and physically during interrogation. You make excuses for their behaviour, still craving their love.

As Schwann took Carter by the arm and left the office, Carter was now back in control of his emotions and ready to play the game. Once on the other side of the door, they briefly looked at each other and shared a split-second moment, simultaneously exhaling, as if they had been holding their breath throughout.

"Congratulations, Staff Sergeant," Carter deliberately said.

"Danke," Replied Schwann, actually quite proud of the words just spoken by his prisoner.

Game on, thought Carter, who in his mind, had just started to initiate a reverse Stockholm Syndrome by hoping to turn Schwann from captor to friend.

After all, honey attracts more flies than vinegar.

Carter managed to grab some sleep but not enough. He mentally ran through what he had been carrying when he took his dog, Fizz, out for a piss last night. An indestructible Nokia 3310, which he had charged that morning, so he should be good for three months of battery life, he briefly chuckled.

Oh, how he wished he could be annoyed by another bloody call, just one more time. Then, he had his wallet with modern currency and bank cards made of plastic (the first not issued until 1967 by Barclays, so some time away) clothes with labels and his Rolex submariner that wasn't first produced until 1953. A fucking awkward day lay ahead. Sleep eluded him.

Chapter 22
Jayne Visits Ho8

Back in real time, Mallory sat in his office with a brew and another he had made for Jayne.

"Seems quiet, Boss, without the banter and bad jokes."

Mallory looked at her knowingly. "Yes, I think so too. I promise you one hell of a piss-up when this is over!"

Jayne's eyes flicked across instantly and a smile spread across her face. "You just swore, Boss, that's the first."

"Yes, I know, Jayne," Mallory said smiling, "let's get to work shall we."

"Well, let me brief you in, Jayne. It appears our cousins across the water have been developing technology that we believed was years, if not decades away and well done them. In short and despite, the fact RAF Menwith Hill had a football pitch array of Cray computers, crunching the data and arguably the largest electronic surveillance capability in the world. The NSA has developed a quantum computer which can calculate the data Menwith is currently working on, not in months, or weeks but in hours. Truly amazing."

"The short story is that *The Event* was triggered by an unfathomable interaction between gravity and tachyons, a particle which until now was considered a theory. But data crunching by the NSA confirms it does, indeed, travel faster than the speed of light and was active, according to the geostationary satellite over Jersey, at the time of the event."

"The upshot is Einstein's theory of relativity, indeed classic physics has been turned on its head, hence, the baffling fact that we can communicate with Tom and the team in real time notwithstanding they are decades in the past."

"Apparently, time and everything that has, is and will ever happen exists simultaneously. The capability of a tachyon is the fluid way in which it moves through the simultaneous layers of time. Once harnessed, a tachyon bond cannot be broken."

"A tachyon doesn't care where you are, how deep or high or indeed which level of time you are in, it will always be with you. So, comms remain real, and so would your mobile phone if you had one to knowingly travel into the past with. It is a fact Jayne; we can communicate with Tom and the team and in theory we could give Carter a bell."

"Imagine the roaming charges on that one, Boss," Jayne said, trying to absorb the information whilst crouching forward on a chair, mug clasped between both hands.

"Our current problem is that Carter has been captured and is presently incarcerated in Ho8, the Jersey War Tunnels as they are now. Tom and his team are on plot but cannot take any action against such a well-fortified position but thanks to the mystery that is all things tachyon, our satellites can observe the terrain for movement."

"Jayne, it's a long shot, but I want you to recce the area within the tunnels where Carter would have been held, I know we are decades in the future but anything is worth a shot."

"Authority has been granted and you cover story is that of a member of the cold case investigation branch of the War Graves Commission. Your antecedence and professional accreditations have been added to the WGC internal database and you are bulletproof on this one."

Chapter 23
Ho8 Jersey, 1944

No one came. Carter waited in his cell at Ho8 to be removed. Nothing. Stress lapsed into boredom, and he found himself on his bunk, on his side facing the natural damp stone wall of his cell.

The reason no one came was because Von Wolff had no words for what lay on his desk.

Von Wolff sat at the commandant's desk. In front of him were items that he struggled to describe. His mind whirled.

What the fuck is a Nokia what are the buttons for and what is it made from? It feels light but strong. What is this rigid cardboard with a black stripe on one side and the name HSBC printed on the front with numbers? This money? English but not their currency and the coins, the receipts in the wallet and the dates on them.

At 08:00 hours, Staff Sergeant Schwann brought the prisoner to Von Wolff's office. Carter appeared and absorbed every detail in the hope of deriving some sense from this dystopian nightmare.

Von Wolff stood up from his desk as Carter was brought in and leant on the desk with both fists. "Who the fuck are you?"

No reply.

"You are a spy!"

No reply.

"I will have you fucking ripped open slowly until you tell me everything I want to know. Believe me, I have done this before to Jews and captured allied troops and airmen, even the wounded. I always get what I want."

No reply.

Here we go, thought Carter.

"But I will have to save that pleasure for another time," said Von Wolff, leaning into Carter's face. "Believe me, I will."

Carter said nothing. In his mind, he thought, *No chance of being the grey man in this situation, just resist until you can't. And when you give up the clock is counting down until all useful intel has been obtained and you are useless alive. No rescue is coming, but if you believe you are now in the past and to protect the future, die before you divulge.*

Von Wolff could not resist his violent instincts and kneed Carter hard in the groin. The only positive upshot was it caused Carter to launch his stomach contents over the captain in an unavoidable and impressive spray of puke.

Von Wolff dry gagged and Schwann inwardly smiled at his superior's evident discomfort as he swept past both to clean up. Carter, despite his genital discomfort, could not help but chuckle.

"Apologies, Staff Sergeant."

"No problem. Good shot," came the smiling reply.

Small *steps*, thought Carter, *small steps*.

Carter remained incarcerated at Ho8 for the next three days. Von Wolff only trusted Staff Sergeant Schwann to act as Carter's jailer. During this time, Carter quietly worked on Schwann, making little probes about his time in Jersey, his life before the war and such without overtly asking tactical questions. And it worked.

One morning, Schwann came into Carter's cell with half a Bratwurst sausage and a slightly warm mug of truly awful coffee and gave it to him.

"I have seen the muck you are given, and I wanted you to have this. At least, to keep your strength up, until you are moved."

Zero to 100 in a Nano-second.

"Moved to where?" Carter said. "Well, firstly Paris, and then, Germany. I cannot say exactly where, but I am guessing SS Headquarters."

"Danke, Staff Sergeant," said Carter, as he mentally worked the problem. *Oh fuck, surely not.*

A short while later, Von Wolff and Schwann entered Carter's cell.

"It is time to leave. Before we go, I must take a photograph of the prisoner for SS records," Von Wolff said. "Unterfeldwebel, Schwann, hold the prisoner whilst I take his photo."

These words alone caused Carter's heart to race; he couldn't help it, and then a wave of hopelessness momentarily washed over him. Carter took one last look at his cell in particular his bed.

I hope to God somehow the message I have left can help me. Then, looking at the camera he stood tall and looked directly at the lens, shoulder to shoulder with Schwann. *Maybe one day someone might find this, recognise me and bring my soul to rest.*

Then, the flash went off on Von Wolff's camera.

As Carter was escorted out of the complex to an awaiting Kubelwagon, a few minutes later, Colonel Schmidt was led away by Von Wolff and pushed towards a truck.

"Take this scum away. I hope you packed some thick socks," he said laughing.

Briefly, Schmidt's eyes met Schwann's. Schwann breathed out slowly and took it all in. With the wire spectacles, the heavy case carried in both hands, the Colonel simply looked like a lost child. Resignation and sadness.

A few Wehrmacht troops on duty walked up to their Colonel to give what frugal words of hope they could. Von Wolff looked at the pathetic display as he drove away.

Chapter 24
Jersey Airport, 1944

The JU88 gently rose off the runway at St Peters airport which had only been opened in 1937. As he sat manacled to a cargo shoe on the floor, Carter listened to the deafening drone of the aircraft going flat out to the French coast.

Well, at least, they didn't worry about excess baggage and thank fuck my tray table was in the upright and locked position he thought, trying to lift his spirits.

Tom and the team, watched the JU88 rotate off the runway and out of sight. Time to go with the intelligence and get ahead and wait at SS Headquarters in Berlin.

Von Wolff, Staff Sergeant Schwann and Carter landed as a priority mission at Paris-Le Bourget Airport. The airport had been Paris' only airport, until the construction of Orly airport in 1932, and so, was heavily defended. This proved to be good fortune for Tom and his team.

As the JU88 gently rose off the runway at Jersey, he and his team were left thinking, *what the fuck now*.

As with everything, guile and self-belief can intimidate anyone and in this guise Tom, Austin, Nick and Jim went on the blag.

Austin was a fully qualified, multi-engine pilot and fluent in German. As the four of them stood before the rather intimidated junior despatch officer in their SS uniforms, Austin demanded to know the route the JU88 was taking.

Provenance smiled upon them and Austin walked out of the despatch office, carrying an authority for the use of a Heinkel HE-111 and the flight plan for Carter's flight.

As Tom and the team strapped into the HE-111, Austin went through the pre-flight checks and engaged the primer, set the supercharger to automatic, and then, started the engines. As they taxied, Austin opened the radiator valves fully then as the aircraft accelerated down the runway the veering was controlled by asymmetric throttling.

With ease, the aircraft took off and headed to Le Bourget with covert priority. So, its arrival was only known to the Le Bourget controllers and the Heinkel would be hangared in secrecy.

Chapter 25
Arrival at Paris-Le Bourget Airfield, 1944

The lumbering JU88 landed heavily and was directed to taxi to a revetment away from the runway or any structures to protect it in the event of a hostile raid. The revetment was, as expected, surrounded by blast walls made of sandbags protecting the small ingress into the hard stand.

Austin approached a few minutes later, having gunned the shit out of the Heinkel. Born out of SBS devilment, he told the controller where he intended to park. The controller, aware of the SS crew on both flights, was more than happy to oblige.

As Carter was being led away from the JU88, Austin's Heinkel was rounding on the hard stand and powering down. Tom's team, once again had eyes on Carter; their spirits rose.

Tom, Austin, Nick and Jim disembarked the Heinkel and strolled towards the despatch hut, to confirm their arrival. Tom walked in taking the lead as an SS Lieutenant Colonel (Oberstrumbanfuhrer).

Austin was wearing the rank of a Major, an SS Strumbannfuhrer with both Nick and Jim wearing the two pips of an SS Captain or Hauptstrumfuhrer. All four wore the Nazi pilot wings and all four were very competent fixed-wing and rotor head jocks in real life.

Private Bauer was, as his name suggests, a lad from the farming fields. The sight of four very threatening and high-ranking SS officers walking towards him simply filled him with dread.

"Oh fuck."

The door boomed open as Tom decided to make an entrance to intimidate.

"Have you arranged officers' accommodation?" asked Tom, with no preamble.

"No, Sir, I was not told. I…No, Sir."

Tom let it hang there for a moment. "Well, I suggest you do so now, go."

Private Bauer ran out to make the arrangements. Tom grabbed the JU88 keys and threw them to Nick and Jim. "Take a look, and see what you can find."

Both Nick and Jim walked confidently out of the office and towards the JU88. The aircraft was casually unlocked, and they both entered. Quite simply the word had gone around that the SS were at the airfield. All the Wehrmacht troops simply melted away afraid of confrontation.

This crystallised the difference between the Allies and the Axis powers. Fundamentally, the Axis powers were brutes, thugs and bullies towards anyone who would enquire or challenge them. This was the polar opposite of the approach and general respect shown by allied officers towards their troops and by default towards the many civilian communities they encountered during the conflict.

So, when Nick and Jim strode across, they were feared and would never be asked for ID, permissions or orders. A perfect environment for a covert operative.

For an hour, Nick and Jim meticulously worked through the aircraft and found nothing which would aid the operation. Reporting back, Tom updated them.

"Well, satellite confirms that Carter was removed from the 88 and taken to a very basic holding cell on the airfield. My thoughts are to tactically intervene before he is transported; based on my best guess this would be SS Headquarters in Berlin. A high-value prisoner of this magnitude will not be trusted by anyone outside of the SS." Sadly, Tom was correct in his assessment.

Chapter 26
Departure to Berlin

Von Wolff smiled as the JU52 lumbered off the runway. He despaired at the good Nazi equipment that was left on the ground and used by the Wehrmacht peasants. They were underserving of the gracious leadership and the benevolence Reich offered them.

In the hold, Carter was still emerging from the fog of confusion and shit that would be normal. The disorientation was initially debilitating; no one else in known human history had experienced what Carter had.

Now, Carter, the first ever person in human history to move through time, was hardening his resolve and preparing inwardly to fight back.

Throughout Carter's training, the capture and interrogation phase demanded (not quietly or politely asked) that you separate yourself from the operational objectives and fight back at every opportunity.

That doesn't mean weapons, although that would be good. It might mean passive-aggressive resistance or feigning injury. Carter, for the first time, was marshalling his thoughts and preparing.

Chapter 27
Jersey War Tunnels
Present Day

Jayne drove up to Ho2 (now known as the Jersey War Tunnels) and parked in the visitor's parking, giving a brief nod towards a potential mini-shopping experience at the War Tunnels gift shop.

Jayne met with the director of the attraction and was given a personal walk-through. The sheer enormity of the construction was overwhelming; in terms of lives and material, Hitler personally oversaw the weaponizing and armament of the Channel Islands and in particular Jersey, as they were British territory.

He regarded them as his anchored battleships and fortified them as such, which was to the detriment of the German defences in Normandy and to the benefit of the Allies on D-Day. It was that simple.

On D-Day, the Allies chose to ignore the Channel Islands and pushed on, ignoring the years of fortification, armament and propaganda Hitler had derived from the occupation of these inhabited Islands in the English Channel.

Jayne entered the holding cell that Carter would have been incarcerated in. She touched the cold walls and thought that only a couple of days ago, in one respect, but also decades and a different century ago, Carter had been here. That poor, poor man.

She was left alone by the director to carry out her work and meticulously set about her examination. She was using photographs of the layout of the original cell to orientate herself to the exact position of the spartan furniture at the time of Carter's detention.

The layout of the cell had been faithfully retained as a museum exhibit and after an hour of examining the walls, floor and ceiling, Jayne turned her attention to the bed. She carefully stripped the sheets and packed them on the small table in the corner. The thin mattress was also removed exposing the frame of the bed.

The bed had remained in incredibly good condition despite being made of wood. Jayne lifted the bed (which was surprisingly heavy) onto its side and examined the long edge of the frame closest to the wall. As she did so, her heart rate began to increase; something had been etched.

Jayne took out a portable LED light and placed it on the frame. Sure enough, the initials JC had been scored into the wood. That could only be Carter's initials. Next to it was Von Wolff and a downwards arrow, Schwann with an upwards arrow and ominously SS HQ Berlin.

Jayne took a number of photos, including infrared for examination. After another 30 minutes, she had completed her search of the bed with no other potential sources of intelligence being discovered.

Jayne carefully remade the bed, carefully comparing each stage of its making to the photos she had taken stripping the bed. The end result was that it was impossible to determine that the bed had been remade.

On leaving, Jayne thanked the director and walked back to her car. She scanned the carpark trying to envisage how frightening and disorientating it must have been for Carter.

And then, the thought that Tom had been here too, exposed to the fearful danger of capture made a knot of anxiety grip her stomach. She knew, at that moment, that her feelings for Tom had crossed a threshold.

Chapter 28
RMPSIB Research

The photos sent to Mallory by Jayne arrived instantly, encrypted to a level that even RAF Menwith Hill up in North Yorkshire would need at least an hour to decipher. Luckily, their leviathan capability was not required as Mallory simply clicked Jayne's file and it seamlessly decrypted onto his desktop.

Mallory looked at the photos, and then, picked up his Brent phone and called the Royal Military Police, Special Investigations Branch liaison officer attached to MI6.

"Lieutenant Colonel Muldoon RMPSIB, how can I help?"

"Lieutenant Colonel, how the devil are you? This is Mallory."

"My God, David, so good to hear from you. When are we ever going to that whiskey we've been promising to sink for about 20 years?"

"I can promise you, Derek, that as soon as my current little op is complete, we will take a road trip up to that little bar on the Isle of Skye and do a dram of whiskey from all the bottles on the shelves, courtesy of His Majesty."

"David, just say when? Anyway, old friend, how can I help you?"

Mallory totally trusted Derek and indeed had supported his application as the MI6 liaison officer. Derek was cleared to access Strap 1 to 3 material and had been extensively interviewed and investigated as part of the Direct Vetting process, returning an unblemished history and clearance to the highest level.

Well, let's see how you handle this, my old friend, Mallory thought with a slight sense of devilment.

They would quietly dine out on this moment for decades to come.

Some 20 minutes later, Mallory heard the heavy sigh of air escape from Muldoon as he probably exhaled for the first time since Mallory's briefing began.

"Fuck," was all that Derek could muster, whilst processing the magnitude of the information he had just received.

"David, leave it with me. We have a vast amount of data at our disposal. I will get back to you with the service history of the two individuals post Carter's capture. Call soon." The line went dead.

Mallory decided to have a Bushmills in anticipation of a long night ahead.

An hour later, Derek called Mallory. "David, I've put a brief precis together of the two individuals. Von Wolff was a nasty bastard who was instrumental in sending the commandant of Ho2 to the Russian front where he perished. Von Wolff, however, was never arrested, found or identified."

"Schwann eventually settled on Jersey and opened a little beach café at St Ouen's on the west coast. I won't go into detail, it's all in the report that I have just sent. Catch up soon. Bye, for now."

Mallory lowered the phone and opened the file.

Schwan was clearly just a country boy who had been called up and was thankful that he had been posted to Jersey. Although, in hindsight, it was considered a safe posting during the war, (due to the fact it was British sovereign territory) a prime target for Great Britain to retake, hence the reason Hitler had personally decided to fortify the Channel Islands so heavily. So, at the time, it was a bit of a tense place to be.

Von Wolff was a different kettle of fish. Allied bombing was devastating and none of the archive records from the SS Headquarters at Prinz-Albrecht-Straffe in Berlin, just north of Tempelhof Aerodrome survived. Muldoon was able to draw from captured documents recovered in the camps which painted a different picture of what could be described as a simply evil man.

When Berlin fell, the bombed-out remains of the former Headquarters were subsumed into East Germany along with the supposedly priceless information that survived the Nazi attempts (to what the Allies believed) to burn the evidence of their brutal regime.

What became apparent from Muldoon's research was that Von Wolff was a blood relative to Ernst Kaltenbrunner who ended up being the highest-ranking surviving member of the SS and its final leader. Unfortunately for him, the view was taken that he had a vicarious liability for the actions of the Schutzstaffel and paid for the privilege with his life, sentenced to death by hanging in 1946.

It was a more merciful departure from the planet than the millions his organisation had slowly and painfully tortured, starved and gassed in the abhorrent concentration camps.

The briefing went on to say that Von Wolff had spent his time working up through the ranks of the Sicherheitsdienst (SD) which was the security service of the SS and a feared subdivision of the SS within the SS itself.

He had personally been involved in the investigation and murder of suspected partisan Wehrmacht troops and was instrumental in the organisation of the shooting in 1942, of around 10,000 Jews in Krakow, Poland.

Sadly, Von Wolff was never captured and it was believed that he had managed to travel to Brazil where he spent the rest of his days amongst the German ex-pat community.

Strangely though, he must have completely cut himself off from his family and no one fitting his description was ever picked up by the Austrian Jew Simon Wiesenthal, or later, by his Nazi-hunting operation under the name of the Simon Wiesenthal Centre based in Los Angeles.

Admittedly, Von Wolff, like many ex-Nazis, could have undergone plastic surgery, but this would have eventually come to light.

Muldoon's report confirmed that Von Wolff had been sent to Jersey to carry out an unannounced inspection amid suspicion of growing distrust and resentment of the Fuhrer amongst the German high command in the Islands. Several officers were reassigned to duties on the Eastern Front where none survived.

Mallory closed down the file on his computer and took stock of the implications for the operation. The team needed to know about Von Wolff's history; a man, who by any standards, was evil personified. Maybe, the fact he had vanished without a trace, could work in their favour as it meant if encountered, he could be eliminated without necessarily raising suspicion.

Chapter 29
Sierra 22 Depart Paris Le Bourget Airfield

Tom and the team boarded the HE-111 through the crew door on the starboard side of the fuselage. Simultaneously, they received a brief update from Mallory on the discovery made by Jayne at Ho2 and the subsequent intelligence received from the research carried out by Muldoon.

As Austin powered the throttles forward, and the Heinkel rotated off the runway, Tom's thoughts drifted. Maybe because events crystalise emotions and make you think about what is really important in life.

He realised that he had just taken off in a German aircraft from a German military airfield, dressed as a Nazi, heading towards the viper's nest that was/is SSHQ in Berlin. But in truth, he was just hoping to see Jayne again.

Tom snapped himself out of his reverie as Nick passed him a brew. It was just amazing, Tom pondered, that wherever the fuck they had operated, anywhere on the planet, Nick could without fanfare or seemingly trying just magic up a brew.

"Fuck's sake, mate, how on earth did you manage that!" Tom laughed.

"I'm a resourceful bastard," Nick replied. "The despatcher had a tin pot hanging over a fucking little Hexi-type stove arrangement. So, we spoke about light discipline in a combat zone and I confiscated his hazelnut coffee. Tastes bloody lovely. I've already brewed up for Austin and Jim, the children are loving it."

Tom laughed and inhaled the steam. "This is way better than the boss' hazelnut brew. Any time spent with these boys always made you feel good."

Tom looked at Nick as he turned away to secure the coffee, and then, forward to the cockpit and saw Austin and Jim working hard as the light dropped and night-time navigation kicked in.

It was now Jim's turn to shine as the math involved in navigating at night and with no ground reference, relied on speed and heading calculations; good old time over speed equal's distance.

With marginal input from quite primitive instruments that suggested wind drift, tailwind or headwind you could be literally miles off. This happened on countless bombing raids on both sides.

As Jim worked his slide-rule, Nick leant forward and keyed his throat mike, "Are you able to update us on the JU52's course, direction and altitude? Over?"

"Yes, yes," came the cool American reply. "Tell the guys their math is good. We have it from here. Steer 090, maintain altitude. The JU52 appears to be heading towards Tempelhof Aerodrome. We will be diverting you as there is an inbound RAF Lancaster raid heading towards Berlin."

Tom and the boys smiled. This was so fucking unreal, getting tactical aerial intelligence from a controller from a different continent, diverting them around an inbound RAF Lancaster bomber attack in 1944, as seen from a covertly launched KH-12 satellite in the next century.

The cool American spoke, "Gentlemen, confirming for the purpose of your ingress into Berlin and your egress home you will remain Sierra 22. Good luck, gentlemen, remember the only easy day was yesterday."

Jim laughed. "Fuck's sake, we've got a fucking Navy Seal as our tactical point of communications!"

They were following the JU52 to Tempelhof. As they looked outside, the bursts of flack caught in Nazi searchlights brought home just how treacherous and how utterly brave the RAF crews were in pushing on determinedly towards their targets.

Make no mistake, the young men in those bombers felt alone, scared and vulnerable; some of them had been schoolboys, just a few short months ago.

Nick looked left and saw a Lancaster very close by take flack in the port wing and radioed the team. The wing, despite its rugged engineering simply parted from the airframe. The Lancaster began to spin like an acorn seed, spiralling down.

The centrifugal force created by the spin denied the crew inside any opportunity to escape; it was like trying to walk a straight line on a spinning merry-go-round, just impossible.

For what seemed an endless time, the doomed Lancaster remained in the beam of the searchlight, spinning and spinning, until it passed the lowest point of the searchlight's elevation. For a few seconds, the Lancaster regained its dignity, alone in the dark.

The crew inside must have watched their deaths unfold as the rushing ground sealed the inevitability of their fate. Spinning towards the ground one last time, this once majestic beast and her crew, hit the earth in a bright flash as her ordinance exploded on impact, lighting up the sky in one last act of valiant defiance.

Nick, for the first time in his life, was genuinely shocked by the ineluctability of death that visited that poor crew. He noted the date and vowed, if he ever made it back to find out who those guys were and he will honour their memory. A thought silently echoed by the rest of the guys.

Chapter 30
Tempelhof Airfield, 1944

The JU88 touched down followed by the Sierra 22 in their HE-111. Having witnessed the stark violence inflicted on the RAF their grim resolve now took on a deeper emotion.

This was a hard bunch of well-trained bastards with the moral fortitude that was engrained within the UK Special Forces community. Tom spoke to the team as Austin parked the aircraft on the hardstand as the engines wound down.

"Gents, up until now, this has been almost surreal, like watching a movie. In the past, well the future, we have all lost mates and seen death and taken life. But I think the fact we saw the crew of that Lancaster go down tonight has brought our mission into hard focus. We always knew this was going to be different."

"We are amongst one of the most brutal regimes that the planet has ever suffered. We know from history that millions of innocents were being slaughtered in concentration camps. We are there now! Hundreds are dying as we speak, every minute of every day."

"Guys, as of this moment, our normal rules of engagement are dissolved. We do not wait to be fired upon until we fire, we take the initiative. Make no mistake, any flicker of compassion must be extinguished. If we fail in our mission, the war could be lost."

"We need to prevent Carter from giving up any intelligence to those bastards and by that, I mean, the World War II history lessons that you would expect him to remember from school. They are, now, fucking tactical gold dust."

"Carter is one of us, he would never willingly give this up, and I'm sure, he would pray to die before he did, as he would clearly know the fucking massive implications and consequences if he did."

"But through interrogation or torture, the huge tactical knowledge that he has inside his head would undoubtedly be harvested. That means, he could change the outcome of the war or to be precise our futures."

"There has never been a bigger mission in human history and we, gentlemen, are at the sharp end. We are the decision-makers; the blunt instruments and we have a fucking job to do and we will finish the job by any means we see fit."

"If we can bring Carter home we will. But, if the situation becomes a stark choice between ensuring the Nazis remain unaware of D-Day, we will make the right choice and ensure history remains unchanged. And we will do so until the last man standing falls. Those are my orders, and I carry full responsibility for any actions this team conducts. Right, let's fucking crack on."

Unbeknown to Tom, his comms (by mutual agreement with the Americans) were live.

Both sides of the Atlantic now concurred with Tom's in-combat assessment.

Tom keyed his mike, "Boss, are you still able to provide us with tactical rolling satellite imagery as it would save any unnecessary exposure of the team; if we were to conduct conventional surveillance."

"Yes, yes, Tom. Our cousins will provide real-time data."

"Roger that, thanks, Boss."

A short moment later. "Sierra 22, we have eyes on your position and the subject is being taken from the JU52 to an awaiting Kubelwagon with armoured escorts front and rear," said the cool American voice.

"Thank you," Tom replied. "For ease of reference, we will refer to you as CAV, short for Cool American Voice and for that privilege, you will be buying the first round once we are back."

"CAV to Sierra 22, it will be an honour, Bro!"

Carter stepped into the Kubelwagon together with Von Wolff and Schwann. Von Wolff just sat in the front passenger seat angry and excited at the same time. He was angry because he hadn't been allowed to kick the shit out of his prisoner but excited that within the hour he could.

Schwann was sitting next to Carter and knew what would soon be happening. Whilst looking directly ahead he strained his eyeballs right and looked at Carter. Carter didn't react. He too knew what was coming. Instead, he focussed inwards and prepared, just as he had been taught.

The journey was only a matter of 20 minutes. Carter vaguely recognised the general layout from time spent in the Royal Marines and later the SBS on training assignments.

As they approached a junction that he recognised, he looked right to what would become Checkpoint Charlie on Zimmerstrabe. He'd been there on a visit on one of the many trips to Berlin during his military service.

Unfortunately, they turned left onto Niederkirchnerstrafe, and then, into the SS Reich Security building; the darkness and the never-ending cold drizzle only added to the psychological blanket of fear that enveloped Carter.

Upon arriving, Von Wolff arrogantly stepped out of the car, scanned the courtyard and marched into the guardhouse.

One blagged Kubelwagon later, and under the guidance of CAV, Sierra 22 was en route only a minute behind.

If only Carter knew, we were this close it would keep him going. Now how the fuck could we do that, Tom pondered.

Almost subliminally the motto of the SBS leapt into Tom's head: *Not by strength, by guile.*

Sierra 22 swung confidently into the compound of SSHQ, Berlin and parked directly next to Von Wolff's Kubelwagon and Carter. Tom assessed the opportunity to extract Carter, but at that moment, heavy anti-tank barriers closed off the entrance. It was getting close to showtime, but not just yet.

Tom leapt out of the Kubelwagon and leant across and said to the Schwann, "Fuck off, and get me a coffee."

Petrified at the intensity and physical presence of Tom, Schwann literally ran to the guardroom. Tom knew he had seconds before Von Wolff would be in his face.

"Carter, you are not alone. Remember the Falklands, remember the Twin Towers. We are here to get you home. We are SBS. Not by strength, by guile."

Tom moved away as if uninterested waiting for Schwann to bring him his coffee.

Carter's head was spinning. A fucking SS officer had just spoken to him in English and told him of two events: one in 1982, and the other in 2001, both decades in the future from his present reality. And then, finished by giving the motto of the SBS. The SBS were not officially called such until 1987 but had lived in spirit since 1944.

As Von Wolff approached, he aggressively shouted towards Tom telling him to get the fuck away from the car. Tom slowly turned and faced Von Wolff, who had, by now, closed to within a few metres of Tom.

As Tom stood, he drew level with and then, looked down upon Von Wolff as he looked up at this beast before him, who outranked him as an SS officer.

Tom leant forward and down. "Fuck off, Hauptstrurmfuhrer and address me as Oberstleutnant. I am your fucking superior!"

Von Wolff, for the first time in his life, felt scared. "I…I am sorry, Oberstleutnant. I have a very important prisoner to deliver for interrogation. It's been a long few days, Sir."

Tom switched into full oppressive bastard mode; a technique used to interrogate prisoners who once intimidated others but were now captured—interrogators turned prisoners. One archetypal piece of shit stood before him.

The beauty of this particular interrogation method is that once the bully is stripped of their power, psychologically, they are in the wilderness in terms of their mental state. Out of their comfort zone, exposed, alone and without exception scared by the shock of confrontation. The harder the shock, the deeper the confusion.

"So, what the fuck are you doing here, Fotze? Leaving your prisoner in a car with one fucking guard? And you say, he is very important! And you, fucking leave him with one guard? You are a fucking incompetent, fucking idiot! Go inside, find out exactly where your fucking important prisoner will be held and report back to me…NOW!"

Schwann who was walking back in Kubelwagon watched with amused detachment as the very word that prick had used against Colonel Schmidt was now coming home to haunt him. From a distance, Schwann could not help but look at Carter and smile.

Von Wolff was almost shitting his pants and burning with embarrassment as he stood before the Oberstleutnant; he knew people could hear the Oberstleutnant's incandescent diatribe. He, very briskly, walked to the guardroom. He wanted to run but he tried to retain some dignity from that fucking awful encounter.

Von Wolff slammed the guardroom door as he entered the compound building, his heart was racing. He was scared and humiliated, but as with all bullies he wanted to hurt the bastard that had humiliated him. Him! For the first time in his life, Von Wolff was scared but his ego was demanding revenge.

Chapter 31
SS HQ Berlin, 1944

Carter's head was still spinning from his encounter with Tom. He did a self-hippy-like diagnostic. No head injury, no drug-like cold turkey hallucinatory events. Christ, it actually bloody well happened!

Carter looked down and smiled. "I can take a kicking and I will fucking prevail because I know my fucking muckers are here looking out for me. Fucking bring it on!"

Tom's words had done the trick and despite the time disorientation, Carter's training had kicked in and he was accepting this reality and digging deep. He was once again, an SBS trooper and a calm and angry one at that. Carter had a lot of aggression to burn off after the loss of his wife.

He really was not someone, an enemy would ever wish to experience. Unluckily, Von Wolff had opened that little bottle and the professional, aggressive, intelligent and deadly Genie was out; try messing with that fucker at your peril.

The door slammed open and Von Wolff walked in followed by Schwan. Von Wolff was not comfortable having been so savagely castigated by Tom. He was emotionally disorientated having to deal with the sublime effect of embarrassment. In his head, everyone had seen what happened and was laughing at him.

But in this case, he was wrong, only a handful had seen the show, but word spreads around bored troops pretty quickly. The effect of Tom's calculated performance was having a massive impact on Von Wolff's ability to operate objectively.

Sitting quietly in Tom's Kubelwagon throughout were Austin, Nick and Jim. Nothing was said but cold glances were exchanged. Tactically they were ready at a moment's notice to unleash controlled violence.

They had brought 21st century weaponry with them, they also had decided to employ the use of body armour. Not the bulk standard stuff any Walt could buy, but the very top-end SF kit.

Their senses were screaming to get out of this fucking tin can and find a more tactical position to defend themselves, if it all suddenly went noisy. Alas, they had to remain seated looking bored and uninterested. The team could feel that the tempo was hotting up. Very soon, it was all going to kick off.

Von Wolff walked towards Tom, having regained some of his composure, ramrod straight and exuding his trademark air of arrogance. "Oberstleutnant. Sir, the prisoner will be taken to the basement level of the SSHQ on Niederkirchnerstrafe for interrogation. I will personally be carrying out the interview, shall we say." Von Wolff laughed as he held his leather gloves and slapped them across his opposing palm.

Unbeknown to Sierra 22, Von Wolff had raised suspicion with the guard commander and the airfield, that he, as a senior SS officer did not recognise the Oberstleutnant who had so humiliated him, whom Von Wolff felt should have known. An alert was now placed on the Oberstleutnant and his aircraft.

"Very well. I will have my officers escort your prisoner. I do not trust you." Tom leant forward and whispered, "You need to earn my trust. I am sure, that as an SS officer, you will."

Von Wolff surprised himself by somehow feeling proud and motivated by Tom's words. Inwardly, Tom was smiling. Dog training 101.

Carter was passive as he was led from the vehicle and into that baroque and yet somehow austere entrance of SSHQ. This heavily ornate entrance adorned with draped swastikas, eagles and other Reich symbols of power and wealth was designed to intimidate anyone entering whether friend or foe.

Carter looked around knowing that he was, by announcement, up for a fucking shit time at the hands of Von Wolff. He drew comfort that the two hard-looking bastards holding his arms were brother SBS operatives.

Carter was ex-SBS that bond never broke, and so he, and his muckers, were going in with only each other to count on. Nick and Jim on either side were thinking the same thing.

Chapter 32
The Basement Interrogation Level, SS HQ

They all entered the basement holding area, which once would have been called a dungeon.

"Very fucking quiet in here, Hauptstrurmfuhrer," Tom said, addressing Von Wolff.

Von Wolff stood arrogantly, ramrod straight, having regained his composure. "Sir, we have had a clear-out of the degenerative scum, and they have been transported to Tempelhof Station, and then, on to one of the Reich processing facilities. It's so perfect!"

Tom feigned a laugh and slapped Von Wolff on the shoulder; Von Wolff puffed out his chest in a state of respect and pride. The dog training continued.

Carter was roughly handled by Nick and Jim into the basement, Austin was now close and sharp in the backup. "Hauptstrurmfuhrer, I will take this piece of shit into his cell and tell him who you are and what is about to happen to him. Don't let me down."

Von Wolff was fit to burst. "Jawhol mein, Herr!" or translated, "Yes, Sir!"

Dog training complete.

Tom threw Carter into the cell as Von Wolff looked in.

"Hauptstrurmfuhrer, please indulge me in some enjoyment and privacy before you steal all the fun!" Tom smiled.

Von Wolff beamed back. "Please, don't kill him quite yet, leave some for me, Sir."

Chapter 33
SS HQ Holding Cell

Tom walked into the cell and gave Carter a Hollywood-style slap across the face. The wink Tom gave just before allowed Carter to give a five-star response. Von Wolff laughed as he watched via the concealed cameras.

He turned to the guard on duty and simply said, "Fuck off."

A command responded to in very short order.

Alone in the command room Von Wolff flicked a switch, activating the covert microphones.

"So, stay calm Carter and play along. We'll be fucking away from here and homeward bound in no time," said in perfect English.

Von Wolff's eyes widened as he thought the worst! *Fuck, no way!*

He reached forward to press the general alarm and stopped as the cold steel of the Wellrod silenced pistol tapped twice on his right temple. The weapon only had five rounds and was genuine to the era.

Austin crouched next to him and whispered in English, "Yes mate, your fucking worst nightmare."

And as a show of intent, Austin rolled the barrel around Von Wolff's forehead and against his right ear and fired a round through the lobe. Von Wolff screamed in pain, the guards outside laughed at what they thought was the interrogation inside.

Nick and Jim entered the cell to get Tom and Carter out, as Carter passed them both they gave Carter a slap on the back and, "Well done, mucker."

Austin grabbed Von Wolff as he was a massive compromise to their operation. Austin considered killing Von Wolff but reneged as he might have information useful to their extraction. He'd happily shoot the cunt when he was of no use.

Austin grabbed Von Wolff and called for backup over the net. All clicks received. As Nick and Jim entered the command room Von Wolff was being dragged backwards by Austin struggling and thrashing around.

By sheer fucking bad luck, Von Wolff's heel hit a panic button on the desk and the world erupted in a cacophony of claxons and flashing lights. Austin tightened his hold on Von Wolff until he passed out.

The damage was done.

Tom keyed the mike, "We have Carter with us, uninjured. SSHQ is a hellhole but all the prisoners have been moved out, poor bastards. It is only occupied by SS personnel. We are heading to Tempelhof with one German Hauptstrurmfuhrer and one German Unterfeldwebel, a staff sergeant from Jersey; the latter is a good guy. The rats are pouring out of SSHQ, it needs taking out."

CAV came on the net, "We hear you, bro. Make to Tempelhof. We have a modified MOAB inbound to target SSHQ. You need to get out of there asap."

Tom turned to the team. "They've got a modified GBU-43/B Massive Ordinance Air Blast, a fucking MOAB inbound. Time on target, four minutes. Fucking go!!"

Jim gunned the 1,131cc engine (which would just about outstrip a lawnmower) giving no confidence to the SBS operatives. Von Wolff and Schwann were blissfully unaware of their impending doom whilst trying to escape in this fucking go-kart.

CAV came back on the net, "Release, release, release. Gentlemen, the blast radius for the modified MOAB is 1/3 of a mile. The target is SSHQ and you are still there. Can I remind you, gentlemen, that a mile is 5,280 feet?"

"You need to bruise metal to the pedal, gentlemen, and make 1,760 feet in under a minute. Time on target is now 6-zero seconds, 3-zero seconds, 1-zero seconds…God bless you, Sierra 22."

Tom directed Austin to throw the Kubelwagon into a ditch leading into a quarry. They all decamped. Carter pulled Schwann into the ditch.

"Fucking cover your ears, Herbert. This is going to be big, mate."

At that moment, having slid out a modified GBU-43/B was transitioning through time and locked onto SSHQ, guided by the KH-12 satellite in geostationary orbit above Jersey.

The sonic boom as the bomb descended was the loudest thing ever heard on Earth. Then silence. Light travels faster than sound. The next thing, the team experienced, was a blinding flash, followed a few seconds later, by a boom that reverberated through their chests and drummed on. The blast was devastating.

Then, silence fell. The quarry had sheltered Sierra 22 as the blast pushed violently overhead. They had failed to escape beyond the blast radius but providence, for once, has shone upon them positively.

Chapter 34
Real-Time

CAV and his team looked at the data in shock. Poor bastards. Satellite confirmed that Sierra 22 was within the blast radius at the time of impact.

The resulting TED (Transient Electromagnetic Disturbance) caused by the electromagnetic field of the ordnance entering the past from the present day had somehow caused the descending bomb to create the equivalent of an EMP (Electro Magnetic Pulse).

This, prevented any real-time intelligence on ground surveillance, obscuring all remote ground imagery; there were no comms with Sierra 22 and their frequency could not be detected.

At Corporate Trading International, Mallory sat back heavily in his chair. "Oh my God." Then, he realised Jayne was in the room, just them listening. "Jayne, could you put a brew on? A long night ahead I think." Words that were said deliberately to let Jayne leave the room to deal with her own grief privately.

"Yes, Boss," came the stoic reply.

Jayne reached the office kitchen and just managed to reach the toilets in time to bend over and vomit into the bowl.

The release of the physical subconsciously allowed the emotional to have its turn next as she crumpled to the floor, grabbed a towel and sobbed into it. "Oh, Tom …please, no."

At the same time, Tom leant down looking at Von Wolff. "You fucking pig!"

Von Wolff spat. "I know from the documents we seized that you are English spies."

"Well, then you need to look behind at what we have done to your SSHQ and your fucking documents," Tom said as he lifted Von Wolff to face the aftermath of the MOAB.

Von Wolff looked back in horror at the devastation. The symbol of his belief structure, his very credo was aflame; SSHQ was no more.

"Yes. But I am still here, and I know and the whole Reich, the whole world will know," Von Wolff said.

Tom looked directly at Von Wolff and said, "You really are a fucking dumb wanker." And jabbed a morphine syrette from a med pack into Von Wolff's neck.

Back in the office, Jayne emerged sometime later, with two mugs of coffee, hoping that the boss couldn't tell that she had been crying. He could.

"Thanks, Jayne. By the way, we have yet to hear any confirmation that Sierra 22 has been harmed. The EMP will be clearing over the modified MOAB impact zone in just under 10 minutes. And our cousins are just as keen as we are to verify their current status. So, Jayne, accept this as a direct order on pain of dismissal," Mallet smiled as he pushed a double dram of single malt to Jayne.

"No negative thoughts, straight into the coffee and drink!"

Despite the uncertainty of the operation, Jayne pushed her emotions to one side and did so, it was actually pretty bloody nice!

Chapter 35
Berlin to Jersey

The airfield was in disarray following the explosion. The old military adage that in combat, all plans are fucked after first contact was so clearly evident.

There was no training, leadership or drills that supported the German troops at the airfield. They were all in shock and operating independently and not as a cohesive fighting force.

Tom and the team watched as the headless chickens of the Reich ran around in an almost aimless search for purpose as they individually tried to process what they had just experienced. Sierra 22 used this to their advantage.

Tom rallied the team. "We are one clusterfuck away from a shitstorm. We need to fuck off now. Any last ground actions?" (Slang for, what have we forgotten?)

They walked towards the HE-111 and entered through the fuselage door on the starboard carrying the limp form of Von Wolff. The air traffic controller looked on, aware of the message he had received from Von Wolff, a man he personally despised.

Notwithstanding this, he took in what he saw and as a loyal German, hit the klaxon. Immediately, the clusterfuck became a shitstorm.

This one action, galvanised the airfield as they could once again embrace a scenario that training had caused them to run time and time again. They were back in their comfort zone whereas Sierra 22 was out of theirs.

Tom keyed his mike, "Everyone, let's get the fuck out of here, all callsigns acknowledge."

Tom received three as expected with Nick confirming Carter and Herbert were onboard, as was Von Wolff.

"Great guys. We will be losing cargo en route. I need a deep sink, no trace. Search the plane. Austin, upfront. Nick and Jim, man the onboard weaponry. Carter, keep a gun on Von Wolff and a casual one on Herbert. He is okay, but be careful."

As the HE-111 lifted off the runway at Tempelhof, Von Wolff was coming out of his heroin stupor. He was sat in a canvas bag for fuck sake which had cargo chains at the bottom.

Carter leant into Von Wolff and said, "Fancy a swim, mate?"

Von Wolff screamed as he rocked back and forward in the sack, his hands cable-tied with plastic yet to be invented.

"Fuck you! Fuck you!"

As the HE-111 rotated off the runway, two ME109s that had recently landed at Tempelhof to refuel came to life as the ground crews started their engines in anticipation of the pilots scrambling.

Within minutes, Oberstleutnant (Lieutenant Colonel) Michael Krauss and Hauptmann (Captain) Eric Von Miller were strapping in with orders to intercept, and if possible, force the HE-111 to return to the airfield or shoot down the aircraft.

Both pilots had glanced at each other, frowning with puzzlement at these orders as they knew they were piloted by and carrying SS personnel. But orders are orders.

Krauss felt totally desensitised after years of war, first providing fighter air power during the Spanish Civil War in support of General Franco's nationalist forces, and now, fighting against the inevitability of the allied invasion and defeat of the Reich. He just wanted to go home.

Von Miller, on the other hand, was full of Nazi piss and vinegar and relished combat. In the final analysis though, it wasn't really combat but attacking vulnerable targets like the little boats or the soldiers on the beach at Dunkirk awaiting evacuation. Or clipping the parachute lines of a pilot or aircrew member after they had bailed out and watching them plummet down.

Krauss had seen Von Miller do this and had fucking pinned the cunt to the crew room locker and threatened to fucking kill him. But here they were again.

Krauss just hoped no more atrocities would happen, *Please, God. No more.*

Von Miller offered to take the lead as the pair left the runway and ascended towards Sierra 22's altitude and heading.

Within the HE-111, Sierra 22 was receiving live threat intelligence from CAV, "CAV to Sierra 22. Sierra 22, you have two hostiles inbound, you are heading 270 degrees they are 090 degrees as you look down your tail and inbound."

"Sierra 22 to CAV. Thank you, CAV. Can you detail altitude and heading as we have a rear-mounted rigid MG34 in the tail assembly?"

"CAV to Sierra 22, yes, yes."

"CAV to Sierra 22, hostiles are at your altitude. 1,000 m and closing."

"Sierra 22 to CAV. As soon as the hostiles break 400 m, let me know. We have 7.62 mm ready to meet and greet."

"CAV to Sierra 22. A secondary hostile has broken off and is heading on a return route home. Intelligence indicates he has a fuel issue and may have to bail out but is making for the runway."

"CAV to Sierra 22. Hostile is 500 m, directly behind you at your exact height. Now, 450 m. Sierra 22, hostile is at 400 m."

As Von Miller closed in, he was euphoric at the thought the fuckwits in the lumbering piece of junk ahead could not see or hear him approach.

Maybe, a bit more chute snapping tonight, he laughed.

At that very same moment, the MG34 in the tail unleashed its spears from Mars. The rounds penetrated the engine, wings and cockpit of the ME109 tearing into the airframe as Von Miller was ripped to shreds.

In his death spasm, Von Miller had squeezed the button on his control column, which before the demise of the ME109, had fired off only two rounds: one of which had clipped the hydraulic reservoir of Sierra 22's HE-111 which was now slowly, very slowly leaking fluid.

Sierra 22 went feet wet an hour later as they breached the French coast heading towards Jersey.

Tom stood up and walked aft from the cockpit. Von Wolff was still cable-tied in the canvass sack. Herbert was asleep and Carter was awake as soon as Tom emerged.

Fucking top bloke, Tom thought.

Tom leant down to Von Wolff and said, "We are minutes away from letting you go. Do you want to say a prayer before you die? Maybe God will take mercy on your soul." Tom slapped him across the face. "Did you hear me?"

Von Wolff could not comprehend his death and remained silent, hoping the voice would go away and he would once again be at home. Tom handed Von Wolff to Schwann who had been woken by Carter.

Schwann leant over Von Wolff who blinked slowly and looked up at Herbert, scared and overwhelmed with fright at the inevitability of his impending death.

In a fleeting moment, he remembered watching others cower before him in the same manner. They knew he was their killer and at the same time, felt powerless, scared and vulnerable as a little child would. Von Wolff experienced this very moment.

Despite this, the memory of his power and of taking life sometimes unnecessarily and painfully, made him smile. A truly evil man. He was brought back to reality by a punch to his face from Schwann. The SS Nazi in him ignited. "You, fucking prick! I will strip you of your rank Unterfeldwebel and have you shot!"

Schwann merely leant into the trussed Von Wolff and headbutted him across the nose. Von Schwann howled in pain (an experience he was more used to giving than receiving).

"Funny, how things change," Herbert said as he lifted Von Wolff up and toward the port door which was open.

"This is for Colonel Schmidt. As a garrison, we loved him, but you killed him. Expect no mercy from me."

Von Wolff felt the push, then the rush of air as he fell and fell. No remorse, just self-pity as he fell the thousand feet into the 98 fathoms of the channel abyss.

Carter placed his hand on Herbert's shoulder. "Are you okay, Herbert?"

"Yes, yes, I am," the big German replied. "Thank you. I feel that we have avenged my poor Colonel," Herbert replied.

Tom crouched down next to Schwan and said, "What you just did was completely justified. Never, ever feel any guilt for what has happened tonight. Von Wolff was a violent pig and killed many, many good people, even his own troops. Depending on your belief structure he is in for a bad eternity."

In his head, Herbert shook off any modicum of guilt like a dog after a dip in the surf and smiled. "Thank you. I don't know how to say thank you enough."

Tom leant down and whispered, "I'm not supposed to say, but when you get back to Jersey and when the war ends, you may want to get hold of an old bunker on the west coast in the bay of St Ouen's and turn it into a café."

Herbert laughed. "Yes! When we were on training exercise, I would look across the bay at the surf rolling in and would think this is perfect. How lovely to spend the rest of your days looking at the surf…I love cooking."

At the same time, Zulu 55 lay in wait at Noirmont in Jersey. The educated ones in the head shed had surmised that the point of ingress would be the same as the egress. So, they waited knowing Sierra 22 was inbound.

It was clear to Austin that the hydraulics had been hit and the performance of the flaps, elevators, rudder and controls were now heavy, sluggish and degrading as hydraulic fluid ebbed away. Hopefully, he could maintain a safe course and head with the intention of landing at St Peters Airport in Jersey.

Alas, the slow loss of hydraulic pressure was affecting the ability to use the control surfaces. Time was running out.

"Sierra 22 to CAV. We are inbound, but we are losing altitude and the ability to control our aircraft. We will not make the runway at Jersey."

"CAV to Sierra 22. Roger received. Zulu 55 is at Noirmont to meet you. They were expecting you to arrive after landing at the airport but clearly, things have changed."

"Can you make it to the scrubland of Noirmont? Which, may I remind you, is a heavily defended peninsular of the Island of Jersey."

"Roger that, all we can do is try. I'm going to be too busy for comms, CAV. So thanks for all your help, mate. Sierra 22 out."

"God bless you, Sierra 22. Keep safe."

Chapter 36
London

Mallory listened in with growing unease. The SBS troopers had done their job and were likely to be killed by the German garrison at Noirmont as they attempted to crash landing.

"Not on my bloody shift!" Mallory said as he lifted his Brent phone. "John, there's a problem that we need to fix."

The German emplacements on Naval Batterie Lothringen at Noirmont were well-known to the modern-day population of Jersey having been faithfully restored by a dedicated and self-funding group of local enthusiasts.

They had, through sheer determination and long hard hours of voluntary work, created a living memory of the Island's survival under the Nazi occupying regime.

But now, the decision was made to take out the anti-aircraft and all military positions at Naval Batterie Lothringen, Noirmont. Authorisation had been given to deploy two Apache helicopters that would accomplish the task.

Austin was passing a southerly point of Jersey known as Green Island, ahead he could make out the headland of Noirmont. He now needed to keep the damaged aircraft on this approach and hopefully land wheels up and survive. The only problem was the defensive garrison that would unleash hell and fury should he maintain his heading.

"Sierra 22 this is CAV. We have two Apaches from the Joint Helicopter Command (this was the joint helicopter battlefield command of the Royal Navy, Royal Air Force and the Army) they are ready to suppress enemy fire on your approach."

"Be advised, the best area to land is by a farm at the entrance to Noirmont from the road. Currently, this is the LocStat (Location Status) of Zulu 55 awaiting your arrival and is the designated pickup point (PUP) or will RV with you at any other location you land."

Austin turned to Tom. "I need to get altitude, mate, whilst we still can. Noirmont is approximately 185 feet AMSL (Above Mean Sea Level). I've got no comms with the Germans. So, I can't blag my approach as a damaged aircraft. They'll just unleash. I reckon we are in their crosshairs as I speak."

"CAV to Zulu 55 and Apaches. Apaches, you must take out the anti-aircraft positions now!"

"CAV to Sierra 22, Apaches have crossed over. No idea what the occupying force is going to make of that Wokka-Wokka sound."

Despite everything, CAV's last comment raised a grin on the face of each member of Sierra 22.

Carter looked at Tom. "What's so fucking funny, mate?"

So, Tom told him. "You fucking what?"

On the ground, a strange noise could be heard. It had no source as it was bouncing off the rockfaces of Noirmont due south, and southwest as the Apache's approached.

"Yankee-Zero-One and Yankee-Zero-Two on station," said the clipped British upper-class accent of Flight Lieutenant Mohammed (Mo) Khan. "Callsign it, Smokin'."

Mo always took the piss out of anyone at every opportunity and was a truly well-respected officer in the squadron. Clicks were received.

"CAV to Yankee-Zero-One and Yankee-Zero-Two. The anti-aircraft positions have been identified at the locations being fed into your systems now. You have been allocated your targets. Good hunting. CAV out."

The data swept into the Apache's targeting systems from the geostationary KH-12 overhead albeit in a different century.

"Mo to Tommo. You go."

Flight Lieutenant Tommo Thompson acknowledged and climbed his AH-64D from below the cliff to the south to level with the first set of anti-aircraft positions. A number of German troops watched in awe as the noise of this beast increased as it rose level with them.

The short spin of the M230 chain gun was the last thing they heard before 30mm rounds were spat out with deadly accuracy at 625 rounds per minute.

Tommo's designated anti-aircraft positions were obliterated by the release of Hellfire missiles, guided to their targets by his onboard laser. Once complete, he dipped back down below the rockface and took up a defensive position behind Mo, who was just about to give his targets the good news.

Austin in the lumbering HE-111 witnessed the devastating attack by the two Apache's on the defensive approach to his landing site. Moments before, he had climbed to just over 200 feet; enough for the German defences to have ripped them apart had it not been for the Royal Air Force Apache intervention.

From above, the KH-12 watched the HE-111 just clear the coastal headland and head inland along the Noirmont peninsular. On both sides of the Atlantic, eyes stared down helplessly. Mallory turned to Jayne as if to say *go*. Jayne stayed as everything slowed and became silent as the guardians watched.

The complete opposite was happening in the HE-111. Help was being given to handle the flight controls. Orders were shouted and replied to. A determined crew was trying desperately to keep a dying ship alive. Soon no hydraulic power existed and the plane started to gracefully go in.

Tom shouted, "Brace for impact."

Everyone grabbed anything sturdy to hold on to. Carter looked at Herbert and winked. Herbert smiled back and then blackness enveloped them.

High above the KH-12 confirmed that the HE-111 had gone in. It appeared that the pilot had flared the aircraft at the very last minute, and by luck, had missed a rocky outcrop and in doing so had reduced the speed of the HE-111 but still probably too fast for anyone inside to survive.

The post-impact silence was almost deafening Herbert thought as he drifted back into consciousness. He looked around. Carter was motionless as were Tom, Nick and Jim. A wave of grief washed over him. Please no.

A bang on the door made Herbert jump as it slammed open, and Ash looked in covered by his Zulu 55 team.

"You must be Herbert," said Ash, looking down at his 21st century weaponry, as Herbert looked up at the same barrel with wide eyes.

Ash swept the fuselage entrance with his Heckler & Koch HK417 assault rifle (with the butt folded by choice).

"On your knees, Herbert! Turn around and cross your legs behind you! Now lace your fingers behind your head! I've heard good things about you, but fucking move, and I'll blow your head off. Are we clear?"

"Crystal," replied Herbert.

"Correct answer, mate," Ash said and patted Herbert on the shoulder as he entered the dark fuselage.

One other trooper swept in as smooth as glass without a sound, sweeping his HK417 across all arcs of potential fire in almost a balletic performance of controlled and restrained violence. Herbert had never been so scared.

"Aircraft secure," the trooper radioed. "All external arcs covered. No sign of troop movements thanks to the rotor heads."

"CAV to Sierra 22 and Zulu 55. Can all callsigns acknowledge?"

Only Zulu 55 acknowledged.

Mallory leant forward at his desk and cupped his brow in the palm of his hand. Jayne, at the same time, just broke down. Her shudders turned to sobs.

Mallory, in his fatherly way crossed to where Jayne was sitting and simply put his arm around her shoulders. "I know. I know," was all he could say before Jayne buried her head into his chest and bawled her tearful emotions out.

"I just can't believe, he is gone. I never got to tell him how I felt—" Then, another wave of grief washed over her.

Back on the ground, Ash was quickly triaging the bodies in the aircraft. So far, Nick and Jim had banging heads (probably as bad as their legendary nights out on the piss at the Prince of Wales pub in St Helier).

Austin was not in a good condition having fought to the very end to save the team as the aircraft went in. His leg was broken. The morphine syrette had kicked in so no pain for the next hour or so.

As Ash approached Tom his heart sank. Tom's contorted body was slumped over the control column of the Heinkel. This part of the aircraft had borne the brunt of the impact.

The airframe had not been torn apart so Tom had not been ripped open as the aircraft crashed, but he was motionless and quickly under stress Ash could not detect any vital signs.

Ash did not have the time to do *any of that John Wayne shit* as was mentioned in the briefing by Tom and Tom was gone.

"Zulu 55 bar one, Sierra 22 are stable casualties. Tom is showing no vital signs. I will white-phoss the body once all Sierras and Zulus are removed from the airframe."

Jayne simply hugged Mallory and sobbed uncontrollably.

Solemnly, Ash dragged Tom's body from the cockpit and into the fuselage and set him down one last time.

Ash gently gave Tom a hug as he went to lay his head softly on the deck of the fuselage. Tom coughed. Ash nearly shit his pants.

Ash rolled Tom over. Tom's eyes were open but unfocussed. No fucking dead body could pull that one off.

In a frenzy of excitement, Ash keyed his mike, "Zulu 55. Save one white-phoss. Tom just coughed. He is alive!"

Radio protocol was momentarily broken across continents and time.

CAV responded, "Fucking yes, Bro!"

The Sierra and Zulu troopers responded in a similar vein. Tom would be forking out some serious beer tokens at the end of this little escapade for sure!

Ash leant over Tom. "Great to have you back, mate. Can you tell me where you are?"

Tom blinked slowly as his eyes focussed and he looked up at Ash. "You're still fucking ugly, Ash. I'm good, mate. Good to see you."

Ash grinned. No need for any concussion questions. "Can you get up, Tom?" Ask asked.

"I can, mate, help me up. Nothing's broken or punctured. I just took a bang to the head."

Ash lifted Tom to his feet. "This way. We're nearly there."

As they walked in the darkness, Ash led Tom to Herbert, who, despite his discomfort, was still on his knees as Ash had left him.

Ash turned to Tom and said, "Just one loose end to tie up before we leave."

As he raised his Heckler & Koch HK417 level with Herbert's head. "No!" Carter shouted.

Ash lowered his weapon and cocked his head to one side, somewhat quizzically.

"Guys. Herbert saved me in Jersey and Berlin. Without his bad coffee and Bratwurst, I would have mentally died. Herbert was instrumental in keeping me alive."

Tom chipped in, "He also killed Von Wolff who had sworn to kill the team. He is okay, Ash. We don't need to kill him."

"Herbert, stand up, mate," Tom said extending his hand and helping Herbert to his feet. "We're going to leave you here alive."

Herbert let out a long breath and simply said, "Thank you."

"When troops arrive, you will need to tell them that we are British Commandoes who took you hostage and were going to use you to bargain with, if, we became surrounded. Tell them that we killed Von Wolff and disposed of his body out of the aircraft. You were next, but then, we were attacked by the ME109s and in the confusion, we forgot about you."

"We tried to shoot you as we fled, but you survived. Are you clear with this story?"

"I am, yes, and thank you again," Herbert replied.

"Herbert, are you right or left-handed?" Tom casually asked.

Somewhat confused, Herbert replied, "Right-handed."

Tom promptly shot Herbert with his Luger in the left arm deliberately missing the bone. Herbert yelped and fell to the floor.

"Sorry, Herbert, but we need to give your story a bit of credibility and that flesh wound should do it."

Herbert grinned, "Danke Schoen, (thank you very much) Tom. I hope you all return home safely."

"Thanks. Gotta go, Herbert," Tom said, slapping Herbert on the back.

As Carter passed, he gently hugged Herbert and simply said, "Thanks, Herbert, you saved my life, mate. I will never forget you."

"And nor I you!" replied Herbert with a smile.

As Ash and Tom exited the crashed Heinkel, Nick and Jim together with Zulu 55 had deployed to form a defensive perimeter.

Tom looked back at the devastation caused by the Apache attack on Noirmont.

Several bunkers were on fire, a couple had cooked off; the internal ordinance of high explosive shells having succumbed to the intense heat within the burning bunkers, causing at first a single shell to explode which within milliseconds had set off a chain reaction amongst the other hundred or so shells.

The confined nature of the blast within the bunkers had caused a massive back pressure which needed to escape. The gun apertures acted like a crack in a glass allowing the force of the devastating explosions to simply rip the roof off each bunker reducing the massive guns inside to contorted, twisted junk.

Dead enemy bodies lay everywhere. There was a strange stillness despite the fury of the burning emplacements punctuated by more rounds exploding. No one else was alive on the headland, apart from the SBS troopers.

Ash keyed his throat to mike, "Ash to Sierra 22 and Zulu 55 on me. We will head towards the RV."

"CAV to Sierra 22 and Zulu 55, a JSFAW Chinook is 200 meters to your south ready to bring you home."

CAV was referring to a Chinook helicopter of the Joint Special Forces Aviation Wing based at RAF Odium in

Hampshire, home to an elite squadron of pilots who supported Special Forces operatives on the most dangerous of missions.

"CAV to Sierra 22 and Zulu 55, satellite confirms that you and the Apaches have now crossed back into real time. Welcome back, gentlemen."

As the Chinook lifted away from Noirmont the scene below was surreal in its peacefulness and serenity compared to the burning hellscape they had moments ago escaped from.

To a man, Tom, Carter and the lads nodded off to the deep throb of the rotors as their minds subconsciously began to process their experiences of the past few days.

Chapter 37
Burying Ghosts

The day was spent debriefing the operation ahead of a cross-partisan debrief between the British and American participants involved in the real-time events. No NSA, no intelligence agencies, just the narrow team involved in the actual operation and their immediate hierarchy, namely Mallory and his US counterpart.

Sierra 22, Zulu 55 and Yankee-Zero-One and Yankee-Zero-Two were going through the well-rehearsed post-incident drills putting each action undertaken by both teams into context. Nothing that was recorded would ever be released to the public. It was simply too scientifically sensitive and to be candid; too bloody extraordinary to be comprehended.

The upshot was that the same level of secrecy would be maintained henceforth into the future as had been applied in the past, going all the way back to Forrester and all subsequent custodians. Any compromise would be dealt with by the same rules too.

After a physically and emotionally exhausting day, Mallory called Tom and Jayne back into his office.

They sat heavily into the sumptuous chairs facing Mallory's desk.

"How are you both coping, now the stress is burning off?" Mallory asked.

"Not too bad, Boss," Tom replied. "It's always the same after a job, when the adrenalin subsides, fatigue takes over. I think we are all justifiably knackered. If anything, it was easier for me to be on the ground as I was too preoccupied to worry about, well, me."

"Whereas you guys would have had too much thinking time on your hands and probably, would have gone through every scenario imaginable on my behalf."

Jayne looked out of the window. Mallory filled the gap in the conversation knowing that Jayne was emotionally caught between professionalism and letting Tom know her true feelings towards him.

Time to take control of this. Mallory thought.

"Tom, things have changed since you were last here for one of my after-hours wet debriefs!" Mallory announced as he slid open his desk drawer and placed an unopened bottle of Bushmills on his desk.

He then placed three tumblers on the desk.

"Sorry, but the budget doesn't extend to a fridge in the desk." Mallory said smiling.

Jayne stood up and said, "Well, I need to go to the ladies room and I shall return with ice cubes. Promise to wash my hands!" With that, she spun around and whisked out of Mallory's office.

"Nicely done, Boss. What do you want to tell me?"

Mallory smiled. "Jayne is in love with you. She bawled her eyes out when we thought your team had been taken out by the explosion in Berlin, and again, when Ash said he thought you were dead after the crash at Noirmont."

"Bloody hell, Boss. Jayne is out of my league. I'd be punching way above my weight."

"Tom, you only think like that because you love her too. Do not compromise this conversation, or I'll send you back to 1944!" Mallory said with a wink.

At that moment, Jayne returned with a little ice bucket.

"So, as I was saying, Tom, since you were last here Jayne now enjoys a Bushmills."

"Home measure, please, Boss," said Jayne as she smiled across at Tom.

An hour later, Mallory excused himself. As he stood he said to the pair, "I think we all deserve some time off. Gather your thoughts as we begin the operational analysis next week. I, for once, will be going to sink some whiskey in the Isle of Sky with an old friend of mine."

"Incidentally, my friend is Lieutenant Colonel Muldoon. In conversation with Derek today, it appears that the operation has affected the past." A long pause as Mallory tried to fathom out the mountain of paradoxes. It was intellectually overwhelming.

"So…Two Russian veterans of the war ended up being demobbed. Nothing unusual with that. One of them Pavel became an artist and made a handsome living through his artwork. His wartime friend Yevgeny went on to become a teacher of physics at a local school."

Tom impelled by the Bushmills said, "Where is this going, Boss?"

Mallory, a logical and analytical thinker struggled with this next bit. "They died, only a couple of years ago. Best friends since the war."

Both Tom and Jayne were looking at Mallory somewhat lost.

"The inescapable fact is that both Pavel and Yevgeny were the Russian operatives tasked with driving the material recovered from Carter out of the German Sector occupied by the British and into the Russian sector. They drove over a tank mine and were killed, at which point, we, the British recovered the items, and so, began the operation."

"Holy fuck!" Tom exclaimed.

"I suggest you two bury some ghosts and revisit Giovanni's. Have a well-deserved good night."

"Well," Jayne said, turning to Tom, "lead on Macduff. Shakespeare by the way, Macbeth."

The evening flowed well at Giovanni's both relaxed in each other's company. Having heard Mallory's fatherly guidance about Jayne, Tom felt comfortable and reassured by his words, often looking at Jayne without hearing her words amidst the cacophony of the bar, amazed that she might possibly love him. Then it was time.

"Scumbag Alley," Tom offered.

"Sure, why not," Jayne replied.

As they drew level with the caved-in hoarding where Jayne had been attacked, they stopped. Jayne looked so tiny and vulnerable that Tom could not do anything but pull her close and hold her. There was no resistance.

And then, unannounced, Jayne began to cry. "I thought I'd lost you."

Tom held her closer as she sobbed and said, "Just the thought of seeing you again kept me going, Jayne." Choking on the words as he said them.

With emotions shared, the depth of love no longer needed to be hidden.

"This is the way home," said Tom, gently taking Jayne's hand and leading her away.

Chapter 38
The Circle Is Complete

Carter had thought about Herbert ever since his return. The guy had kept him going through the most awful and disorientating experience Carter (or any other human) had ever endured.

Out of curiosity, he found the café that Herbert had started, which blossomed under his ownership and to this day, was a surfer's paradise on the beach.

Initially, as a German, he had been resented but that is where his personality shone through, and very soon his *Beach Bunker,* as he named it, became the cool place to hang out.

When the VW Beetle movie was released in the 60s, the surfer dudes began calling Herbert, Herbie and a local legend was born.

Herbert married and had a long and loving marriage. He and his wife were the only couple in the retirement home that were given a suite with a double bed.

Then, as is the way of things, he became a granddad and practically a second father to his granddaughter, Tegan (pronounced in rhyme with Megan), whom he doted upon and regaled her with his stories from the war.

Tegan, a tanned, lean surf goddess, was now leaning over the opposite side of a reception desk built from driftwood which Herbert had collected from the surf.

She was facing away and looking down at the day's bookings have not heard Carter enter. Dressed in his beach shorts, loose t-shirt and trip-flops as he called them because he usually tripped on a slab or any remotely elevated piece of fixed structure when wearing these fuckers.

Guaranteed, and with comedy, timing did just that against the bar, stubbing his toe. A random, "Fuck," was said under a muffled breath as he looked down at his toe.

The door creaked as another customer entered. Tegan turned to greet the customer as Carter looked up from his toes.

Her hand instinctively covered her face as her eyes widened. "It's you!" Tegan said as she barged past Carter leaving another girl to meet and greet customers.

Instinctively, Carter followed Tegan and not knowing why, entered the office seconds after her, to find her crying.

Carter held his hands up with his palms facing forward. Tegan looked up.

"It's you. It's really you," she said crying, laughing and smiling at the same time.

Carter said, "I'm sorry, I don't understand."

Tegan opened a drawer, and fumbling in excitement, pulled out a remarkably well-preserved, but slightly folded photo.

"Here," she showed the picture, her heart was racing.

Carter looked down and said, "That was taken by Von Wolff. That's me and Herbert. I remember thinking just before the photo was taken, that maybe, one day someone might find this, recognise me and bring my soul to rest."

As Carter looked up Tegan launched herself into his arms, her legs wrapped around his waist.

"Granddad always said you would come. He loved you."

Oh my God. Thought Carter. *If I'm dreaming, please, don't let me wake up.*

For the first time, since his wife's death, Carter felt a release that allowed him to feel again; she had let him go to love once more.

As the tide rolled in, Tegan and Carter walked hand in hand across the wide and impressive bay at St Ouen.

Tegan looked at Carter, her hair blowing in the offshore breeze and said, "He told me everything. How he brought you bad coffee and sausage. How you thanked him for his kindness. And then, how you saved him in Berlin and brought him home to Jersey and saved him again from being shot."

As Tegan gently kissed Carter, she said, "I think the circle is complete."

Carter looked out to the setting sun on the horizon; the Jersey surf pounding as set after set of waves rolled in.

At that moment, Carter promised Herbert, "Tegan is safe, Herbert, you have my word. She is mine to look after now."